T0064225

HONOR
AND
POLYGAMY

A NOVEL

OMAR FARHAD

iUniverse LLC
Bloomington

HONOR AND POLYGAMY
A NOVEL

iUniverse books may be ordered through booksellers or by contacting:

iUniverse
1663 Liberty Drive
Bloomington, IN 47403
www.iuniverse.com
1-800-Authors (1-800-288-4677)

ISBN: 978-1-4917-3295-3 (sc)
ISBN: 978-1-4917-3296-0 (e)

Library of Congress Control Number: 2014907271

Printed in the United States of America.

iUniverse rev. date: 5/7/2014

Contents

Chapter 1   The Unplanned Deployment 1

Chapter 2   The Reality.. 7

Chapter 3   Wishful Thinking.. 18

Chapter 4   The Despair.. 26

Chapter 5   The Hallucination 33

Chapter 6   The Grand Escape 41

Chapter 7   Nanawatai 48

Chapter 8   The Bravery.. 56

Chapter 9   The Honor.. 68

Chapter 10 The Guilt..74

Chapter 11 The Separation 84

Chapter 12 Emotional Journey.. 90

Chapter 13 The Underworld 98

Chapter 14 The Bitter Truth 107

Chapter 15 Awkward Moments..116

CHAPTER ONE

The Unplanned Deployment

Nicholas Blake is about to leave his office at the UN. It's around seven thirty in the evening, and the rain is pouring down hard. Nick keeps looking out the window to see if the rain will stop for a moment so he can get to his car and drive home. He's looking forward to relaxing from a long day of work. He finally decides to take a chance and run outside because it's getting late. Suddenly his phone rings. He looks at the caller ID. It's Bob.

What does he want at this hour? I'm done for the day, Nick thinks.

Bob is Nick's immediate supervisor at the UN office and the liaison for Afghan affairs. He's one of the most persuasive and assertive persons Nick has ever known. So naturally, when Bob calls afterhours, Nick knows he wants something done immediately.

"Nick, how are you doing, buddy?" asks Bob.

"Fine," replies Nick. "Is everything okay?"

"Nick, you have to do me a big favor," says Bob.

Nick's heart drops because he knows a favor for Bob is no joke. A storm of thoughts races through his mind. Nick doesn't like surprises. He plans way ahead of time because he wants to be able to do things safely and manage time wisely.

What could he possibly want at this time of the night? thinks Nick.

"Well, Nick, Patrick canceled his trip to Afghanistan at the very last minute, and I have no other option but to ask you to go. Can you please talk it over with Lisa and the kids? It would mean a lot to me. Besides, you're the only person I can trust. You're the only person who has the diplomatic skills to finish the job."

Do you really think it's that simple to just talk to Lisa and take off on a six-month deployment? You must be out of your mind, Bob.

Lisa is Nick's wife of eight years. They met as students at the University of Washington when Nick was a twenty-three-year-old political science major and Lisa was a twenty-one-year-old liberal studies major. They met in Dr. Simon's English class, where Nick noticed Lisa's intellectual skills and the way she actively took part in class discussions. She would raise her hand to ask for clarification and assert her point of view. As carefree and funny as Nick was, Lisa was the opposite, thinking about every question carefully before she spoke. One class session in particular, there was an intense debate about the role of government in the everyday lives of people, and Lisa spoke passionately about the responsibility of everyone to take care of others, the haves having a responsibility to the have-nots. He lost himself looking at her as she spoke. After class, he caught up to her and asked who inspired her thinking. That was how it all started.

"Slow down," Nick says to Bob. "Do you know what you're asking me to do? I just got back five weeks ago. How am I going to explain this to Lisa and the kids?"

Nick has been in Afghanistan for the last six long months. He is the point man, coordinating the United Nation's humanitarian efforts in Afghanistan and previously in Iraq. He, with his diplomatic abilities, is hoping to bring a twenty-first-century way of doing business to Afghanistan, a country that in reality is behind one hundred years if not more. He can imagine the twelve-hour days, seven days a week, reminding him of the movie *Groundhog Day,* where he wakes up every day and it's the same day all over again! Nick has been in and out of Iraq and Afghanistan for the past five years—a repeated schedule of waking up in the morning, eating breakfast, going to meetings, eating lunch, working on reports, and sending daily reports to his boss, Bob.

The reason Nick was so willing to be deployed over the past five years was that he wished to be given an office job right here in New York. Nick is promised to have an office job once he fulfills his overseas obligation of learning on the job. However, Bob is now using his willingness against him. Nick wants to say no, but he really likes his job. He gets paid very well, especially when he's away.

Nick remembers counting each day the last time he was deployed, especially when it got close to coming home. He would count down the days with Lisa and the kids whenever he got a chance to talk to them on Skype. Sometimes he wished he could enter the computer screen and kiss and hug his family and never return to his super-boring routine. Sometimes his kids would have a very brief conversation with him because they were in the middle of a video game and wanted to get back to it as soon as possible. Nick understood that kids would be kids. Other times, his kids wanted to have a long conversation with him.

How can I go back to that? Nick thinks to himself.

"It just isn't fair, Bob," Nick protests. "What's Patrick's excuse?"

"I think his dad is sick or something."

"Can you send someone else?"

"Can you at least think it over before you say no? Besides, whom could I send, anyway? I have only you and Patrick."

"I can't promise anything right now," says Nick. "Give me a little time. I still need to process all this and mentally prepare myself."

"Okay, buddy, no problem. Think it over. You'll be leaving in two weeks. I owe you one, pal!"

"Oh, so you had it all figured out!" exclaims Nick.

Oh, I am so dead. How am I going to explain this one to Lisa? Will she understand? Nick thinks. *After all, we need the money for our new house.*

Nick leaves his office in total disbelief. He is so upset he hardly notices the pouring rain soaking him.

Nick opens the door to excited little Ashley and Fargo.

"Daddy! Daddy! Look what I can do!" Fargo says.

"Wow, nice, little buddy! That's one crazy trick," Nick replies.

Preoccupied, he doesn't even see what Fargo does. How is he going to tell Lisa about his assignment again? *In a tough economy like this, I can't afford to lose a good-paying job,* Nick thinks.

"Daddy, you're not listening!" Fargo says and runs toward his bedroom in a tantrum.

Ashley was born when Nick and Lisa were still dating in their last year of college. She wasn't part of the plan at the time even though they were thinking about getting married soon after graduation. They considered the pregnancy to be a blessing and went on to get married soon after that.

"You look stressed out, honey," Lisa says.

"No, I'm just tired," Nick says as he slides his hand over his newly grown beard and stares at Lisa.

"Oh no you're not!" Lisa says.

"I know, I know. I'm sorry, honey, but I was put on the spot this time," Nick says.

"But you just got back. How long are you going to be gone this time? And what the hell happened to Patrick?"

"He canceled at the last minute, and Bob asked me to fill in for him. I'll be away for six months," Nick says, looking out the window.

"This isn't fair, honey. You promised me last time that was your last trip," Lisa protests as tears roll down her cheeks.

"You can scold me another time, darling. I'm extremely tired," says Nick. "Bob put me on the spot again, and plus, we need the money," he rationalizes. "It's only for six months, and it will pass. We can still talk on Skype. We'll be able to see each other, and I can see the kids, too."

Ashley and Fargo come from their room toward the kitchen.

"What's wrong, Daddy? Mom, why are you crying? Are you guys fighting?"

Nick answers no as Lisa wipes her tears and looks away.

"Daddy needs to go away to work for some time," Nick says as he fakes a half smile.

"No, Daddy, you can't go again!" protests Ashley, putting her head in his lap while Nick remains seated, and Fargo holds onto his arm.

Nick chokes up. He holds both of his kids in his arms, close to his chest, and consoles them. "I'll be back before you know it."

Two weeks go by very quickly, and the disheartening day arrives for Nick to leave once again. Lisa is up early cooking, making Nick's favorite breakfast of hash browns covered with eggs, turkey sausage, coffee with milk, and homemade cornbread. Lisa always tries to make Nick his favorite food before a trip. It's her way of giving him part of their home as he leaves. Nick reluctantly forces himself to go to the bedroom and start packing.

Lisa is lost in thought, thinking about if they will ever have breakfast together again when Nick calls from the bedroom.

"I'm all packed up, honey," he says as he picks his bag up from the foot of the bed. "Have you seen my flashlight?"

"Yes, it's in the top drawer of the nightstand on the right," replies Lisa.

"All the little things we take for granted become useful when you're over there," says Nick and smiles. He gets the flashlight and packs it. *All the other little things that come in handy in a place where uncertainty is the name of the game,* he thinks to himself.

After finishing his breakfast with Lisa and the kids in silence, Nick sluggishly moves toward his bags, which he has placed by the door. He hugs and kisses his children good-bye and walks toward the door. Lisa chokes up. Nick tries to avoid eye contact, gives his wife a quick kiss, and walks out the door. For Nick, this is always the most difficult time. Good-byes are not easy for him, and six months is a long time for him to keep replaying them in his head over and over.

Nick is picked up by an airport shuttle, which has made four earlier pickups. Nick tries his best to not let the deployment get into his head. If he does, the next six months will be next to impossible to bear. During every trip like this, he transforms himself into a robot-like personality, which helps him to keep his emotions controlled. When he returns home, the robot personality naturally drops away on its own.

As the plane takes off, Nick feels like crap. The emptiness in his stomach grows. He imagines how Lisa, Fargo, and Ashley might be feeling or what they might be doing right now. As he looks down and sees the shrinking cars driving on the familiar freeways and the distancing landscape, he realizes he is going to be gone for the next six uncertain months. A sense of emptiness falls on him.

I'm not going to wake up in the morning with my wife and kids, he thinks. I'm not going to take them to school, nor am I going to hear them complain about going to school or their daily rationales for why they shouldn't go to school because they want to stay home with Mommy and Daddy.

Nick gets a panicky feeling for a moment and feels as if he is going to prison for a six-month sentence.

Do I have to be in the same environment, with the same people, eating the same food every day for the next six months? I just got back, Nick protests to himself.

In the course of his flight, he sleeps most of the way so he can kill fifteen long hours with children crying in perfect harmony, one stopping and the next one starting, as if they all agreed to it before the flight.

On most of his trips, when he is on his way home, all the people on the plane look happy and cheerful. But going back to work, the entire traveling population looks sad and depressed, or at least that's how Nick feels.

CHAPTER TWO

The Reality

After a long flight, Nick finally arrives at Dubai International Airport and quickly gets out of his seat. He exits the aircraft's main door and runs through the busy airport to claim his bags. Normally, he spends a night in the United Arab Emirates before going to Iraq or Afghanistan. However, this time around, his flight plan was put together rather quickly.

He looks around and notices the familiar parts of the airport he has gone through for the past five years when working in Iraq and Afghanistan. He needs to leave terminal two right away and make it to terminal one as soon as possible or he will miss his flight.

Nick goes to the usual coffee shop, orders a cappuccino, and calls Lisa to tell her that he has arrived in Dubai and is on his way to Afghanistan. He says good-bye to civilization for the next six months and makes his way to the next flight to Kandahar Airfield (KAF). As he looks around the seating area, he sees nothing but rows of contractors waiting for the same flight as he is. He feels a sense of sadness for all of them and wonders how many have left their wives and children or loved ones.

After fifteen minutes, boarding for the flight to Kandahar is announced. Everyone gets up, starts moving toward the departure gate, and then boards the plane quietly as they are welcomed by the stewards. The somber looks on their faces make it clear that no one seems to be in a hurry to get to where they're going. No one wants to make a connection or talk about anything. Each person is in his or her own world, deep in thought.

Nick sits back in his seat, closes his eyes, and dozes off for a brief moment as the aircraft makes its long takeoff roll on a hot, humid day. He dreams his little girl is running toward him with her arms open wide and her beautiful smile. She is saying something, but he can't hear her. She calls again, but Nick is not able to hear her. Suddenly, he wakes up and realizes he is only dreaming. This dream follows Nick every time he leaves on a long trip.

After two hours and twenty minutes, the aircraft make its final approach to KAF. As the plane descends, Nick's heart sinks. He thinks to himself, *Here we go again! Uncertainty, bad food, and terrible accommodations once again greet me.*

Some of the people who work there at the base get lowered to this depressing bowl for the entire six months of their assignment. Kandahar Air Field is a large area that is fortified by T-walls and barbed wires—a typical military base. As Nick leaves the airport, the logo of the Dubai airliner is the most pleasing thing he sees, disappearing in the distance. Nick has no idea how many flights he will take, how many meetings he is going to attend, and how many provinces he is going to visit in the next six months.

Nick is the last passenger to get off the airplane. The hot, dry, dusty air hits his face, and the smell from the "poop pond," where water gets recycled, reminds him of his last trip. Nick thinks to himself, *I thought they were going to get rid of the poop pond with the new system, but I guess not! I'm not surprised how slow and indecisive the military can be sometimes.*

The smell of the poop pond reminds him of the circus elephant trainer of the past who would place an elephant on a hot surface and play a particular song. The elephant would remember the song and start moving whenever it started playing, afraid of the hot surface under his feet.

Nick makes his way to the baggage claim. Unlike at home or in other civilized countries, his luggage is placed on an ordinary wooden pallet. Nick picks up his belongings in three very heavy US Army duffel bags. He exits through an ordinary plywood door, and his friend Charlie waves at him. Charlie, who is in his forties, gets out of his right-side-steering Toyota 4Runner and greets Nick.

Charlie's first question to Nick is, "Did you get a chance to grab a beer in Dubai?"

"No. My flight to Kandahar was within an hour. Just enough time to get a coffee," explains Nick.

"What a bummer!" Charlie says, disappointed, as if the beer were for him.

"So what's new?" Nick asks.

Charlie laughs and doesn't say anything. They both know nothing changes no matter how much time you spend on a military base.

Charlie drives up to the transit tent. Nick isn't unfamiliar with his surroundings. There is a huge tent with two super-sized air-conditioning units on each side, which are very loud by any standards and are trying to keep the tent cool in the 125-degree dry heat.

It feels like I never left this place, Nick thinks.

Nick asks Charlie, "Can you drop me off by Boardwalk so I can get a phone card and maybe something to eat? I don't want to start with mess hall food right off the bat."

Boardwalk is the famous shopping center on Kandahar base. It is made up of a mix of restaurants, Afghan craft shops, military personnel stores from different nations, and a couple of decent coffee shops. Most of the restaurants are open twenty-four hours a day.

"I'll pick you up at 0500 sharp," Charlie says, dropping Nick off at Boardwalk.

"What for?" Nick asks.

"I'm taking you outside the wire tomorrow. I'm going to meet some contacts," Charlie says.

"But I have an early flight to Kabul the next day."

"Oh, stop whining. It'll only take a couple of hours, and we'll be back in no time. You're not scared, are you, Nick?" Charlie asks with a smirk.

"Oh no. I'm really tired. I need to get some rest before my big meeting in Kabul. Besides, the UN helicopter flies out of Kandahar once a week. I don't want to miss my flight. I don't want to get stuck in beautiful Kandahar for a week!" explains Nick.

"Come on, don't be a chicken! I'll get you back in time to rest before your flight," says Charlie.

"Okay. I guess I can't say no to you!"

"I'll see you in the morning," Charlie calls out to him.

Nick walks back from the Boardwalk. Charlie had dropped his bags somewhere by the tent entrance inside the transit tent while he was away. Although Charlie is in his forties, his adventurous personality has not changed since he met Nick. He is still outgoing, a daredevil, and carefree. For Nick, those days are over, and he's more focused on his family and kids.

Nick walks into a huge tent as he struggles with his oversized duffel bags. He looks around and sees row after row of bunk beds. He reads the sign stating, "Maximum Capacity 270!" He drags his bags in hope of finding an empty bed, but there is none. He puts down his bags, looks around, and sits hopelessly on the duffels.

Nick waits for a few minutes to see if someone's going to leave so he can get some rest. The tent fills many times during a twenty-four-hour span. Sometimes platoons of soldiers come in and occupy bunks for a day or two, and other times various contractors from around the world do. These poor bunks never get a rest, occupied twenty-four hours a day, seven days a week. After Nick waits for two hours, a US Army sergeant packs his belongings, preparing to leave the tent. Nick reluctantly asks, "Hey, sir, are you leaving?"

"Yes, and by the way, I work for a living. Why?" the sergeant asks. Enlisted personnel don't like to be called sir because in the army, sir refers to a commissioned officer, and the enlisted personnel feel they are the ones doing the work, not the officers.

"Well, Sergeant, I was hoping I could crash in your bed tonight," Nick replies.

"Well, it's not my bed, and yes, you can crash in this lumpy bed. Just let me get my things together, and I'll be out of your face in a jiffy," says the sergeant.

"Thanks, Sergeant. I really appreciate it," Nick replies.

"No problem, sir," the sergeant says.

Nick pushes most of his duffel bags under the bed and thinks, *Thank God I'm not on the top bunk; otherwise, where would I put all of my gear?*

Nick sinks into the lumpy mattress and sets his phone alarm to 0400. The scenery around the tent is very familiar—soldiers glued to their laptops watching movies or playing video games as they are trying their best to escape the everyday reality of being in the army and the never-ending Afghan war. Most of the soldiers are on their second or third tour and avoiding eye contact with the contractors and anyone with civilian clothing at all costs. Military personnel believe contractors do not deserve to get paid more because they, not the contractors, are the ones paying with their lives. Contractors enjoy the security provided by the military personnel and get paid in some cases ten times more than a newly enlisted private.

Trash—food containers, urine-filled bottles, and bottled water—litters the dirty, dusty tent floor as far as the eye can see. The strong odor from the tent sealant is unbearable. Some people enter the tent through one entrance and walk through the other as if it were a sidewalk, completely disregarding the 270 people resting. The continuous loud sound from the diesel generator and the loud noise from the air-conditioning unit keep Nick awake for a good while. Finally, the lights in the tent are turned off at 2200 hours. Nick is so tired he passes out within two minutes.

His phone alarm sounds off at exactly 0400. Nick searches for his phone under the pillow. It's dark, and he has no idea where he is. It takes him a good twenty seconds before he realizes he's in Afghanistan, inside a tent with 269 other people.

It takes Nick another minute or so before he figures out what he needs to do next. He has no idea where the showers are. Everyone is still sleeping. Some soldiers who were there the previous night are not in their beds anymore. Nick gets up, puts his baseball cap on, and peeks outside the tent, but he isn't able to locate the restrooms. He walks back to the other side of the tent, peeks out the other entrance, and sees several twenty-seven-foot large containers placed in a row in the distance.

"I think I found it," Nick mumbles to himself.

He returns to the tent and picks up his toothbrush, shampoo, soap, and electric razor. He places them in his shower bag, gets his towel, and walks toward the showers. On his head, he places the headband-type flashlight he'd requested of Lisa before leaving home.It is pitch dark; the military base keeps all of the lights turned off for fear of rocket attacks. Bright lights make an easy target.

It must be at least ninety degrees, and it's only four o'clock in the morning. This flashlight is truly magical in a place like this, Nick thinks.

The strong smell from the poop pond is still fresh in the air and confirms his presence in Kandahar.

11

He uses the toilet stall and notices all kinds of writing on the wall. Some of it is extremely insensitive and offensive, and some of it is really funny. He takes a quick shower and shaves while standing in two inches of water and then walks back toward his friend Charlie, who is already waiting for him outside the tent.

"Hey, Nick, did you get any sleep?"

"Oh yeah, I did. I didn't think I would sleep well, but I was so tired. I couldn't even count to three before I passed out," Nick says with a laugh.

Charlie laughs and says, "We should eat before going out. DFAC opens at 0530." DFAC is the dining facility.

"Okay, but do we have time? I need to make a quick call home. I haven't talked to Lisa and the kids since I left home except a quick call I made from the Dubai airport."

"Sure you can," says Charlie. "We'll stop by MWR before going to DFAC." MWR refers to Morale, Welfare, and Recreation.

"Cool," says Nick.

Nick walks in to MWR, looks around, and is glad not many people are waiting to make phone calls or use the computers this early in the morning. On one side of the room, rows of computers are lined up, and on the other side are rows of telephones, one next to another with no barriers in between. A few soldiers are using the phones, and they don't seem to know or care whether anyone is listening to their private conversation. They are in their own world at this moment. Listening to their personal conversations takes their toughness and masks off of their army personnel shell, and Nick can see human beings behind the uniforms.

Nick picks up a phone and dials his home number. The phone starts ringing.

"Hello! Hello!" says Nick.

"Hello, who is this?" The connection is really bad.

"Honey, it's me, Nick."

"Nick! You had me worried, babe!" replies Lisa with anguish and relief. "Where have you been?"

"I'm sorry, honey. I called you the first chance I got. How are you guys?"

"We're fine," Lisa replies, clearly trying to be brave.

"I'm doing well. I got here safe and sound. I had a good night's sleep. I was so tired. How are the kids?"

"They're doing good. Sleeping right now. They're going to be bummed."

"I'll try calling early next time so I can talk to the kids."

"Yes, and don't wait too long next time."

"Oh no, I'll call as soon as I get a chance. I have to go, honey. I have someone waiting."

"Okay, be safe and stay away from adventures."

"Yes, babe, I will, and kiss the kids for me."

"Okay, bye."

"Bye."

Nick walks out of the MWR quickly because he is aware Charlie is waiting outside and doesn't like being late. Charlie is a man of discipline and punctuality. In his line of work, discipline is what keeps him alive.

"I took the liberty and packed you breakfast since we are pressed time wise. You can eat on the way," Charlie says.

"Oh, I took too long?" Nick replies.

"No, we're right on schedule. And by the way, those in the back are Johnny and Dave. They're watching my back."

"They're not packing much, are they?" Nick asks jokingly, looking at their weapons.

"Well, it's for your protection, too, since you don't believe in carrying one yourself," Charlie replies.

"I don't need a weapon where I work now."

"Hey, Johnny, Nick and I were in the same US Army unit."

Charlie starts a conversation with the boys in the back so Nick can relax and enjoy the ride. Charlie then gives Nick an overview of what is really happening here in Afghanistan. For those in real action, things are different than for people like Nick, who are passing by and working for a different department. He may have an optimistic view of things.

Charlie tells Nick as they leave in an armored Land Cruiser, "Humility kicks in every time I leave this gate. Look around you, Nick. Nothing has changed since we first came here twelve years ago. After spending billions of dollars, the same insecurity, the same people, no positive changes. Constant rocket attacks make you feel like a prisoner here at the base. In ten years of being here, we should have been at least welcomed as liberators.

But at this point, I don't think we've made any changes in Afghanistan. The government will fall within a half hour of the US troops' withdrawal. What have we achieved? I'd say nothing!"

Charlie looks disappointed and somewhat angry at the same time. Nick, an optimistic person by nature, does not want to be persuaded negatively by Charlie, but Charlie proceeds passionately, saying, "We made peace with the warlords, the thugs, and the so-called Northern Alliance. The Northern Alliance was pushed back by the Taliban in the first place for their incompetence and infighting. I think we've created a monster with many thousands of heads representing warlords, a super-corrupt government, and ultimately a super-corrupt society. Buying loyalty with the mighty dollar lasts only so long. It's like using a jukebox. You need to deposit more money if you want to hear the next song."

Nick does not like what Charlie is speaking of. He attempts to stop him from spreading such a negative look of the American efforts, but Charlie is unstoppable in what he wants to say.

"The US will ultimately pay for its own creation. Plowing through the country was easy; holding it is another thing that the US hasn't figured out in the past twelve years. I wish the US government or the so-called policy makers had cracked open some history books and done it differently this time around," Charlie says.

Nick is trying his best to tune out Charlie. He does not believe the United States' efforts are failing, but Charlie insistently proceeds with his heartfelt disappointment.

"Loyalty does not exist in this country. The ordinary people aren't even loyal to their own government. They have to side with the Taliban because at least the Taliban are from their own tribes, maybe their own cousins, and when people are pushed around by the Taliban, they have no one else to turn to. Isn't that sad, Nick?"

Nick doesn't know what to say. After all, Charlie is out there in the city almost every day. He knows what he's talking about.

After forty-five minutes, Charlie pulls the vehicle in front of a row of shops in the city of Kandahar. "As usual, this is the spot where we meet my contact, who's going to give me information on various Taliban leadership and their whereabouts," Charlie explains. "We'll move from here in about ten minutes because it isn't safe for us to stay in one spot for too long."

Charlie points to the next block. "That's where our next stop is going to be in ten minutes. The Taliban have their own method of intelligence gathering. They use taxi drivers, shopkeepers, and laborers to keep an eye out for useful information."

When his contact doesn't show up, Charlie starts moving the vehicle to the next stop. Things seem too calm and unusual on this hot summer day. Charlie says to the boys in the back, "Hey, boys. Subjects usually show up within ten to fifteen minutes. What's happening today?"

"Don't know, Charlie. You can call him. If he doesn't show up within the next five minutes, we should go back to base." Dave sits with his finger on the trigger.

The weather was hot and dry but clear when Charlie and the gang left the base in the morning. However, as the temperature rises close to 105 Fahrenheit, the wind starts to pick up. Kandahar is known for its sandstorms. Day can turn into night in a matter of minutes.

"Okay, boys, stand by. I don't like this," Charlie says as he covers his face with a scarf to protect him from breathing the fine sand. "I'm stepping out to make a phone call."

Nick gets a little nervous as he observes Charlie's facial expressions from inside the car. The air outside is getting darker, and for Nick, there is no escape from the fine sand. Nick starts to cough. He is covered with fine sand in a matter of minutes.

Nick turns around and asks the boys in the back if it's normal for the contact not to show up. A shot rings out, and Charlie goes down.

Dave and Johnny start screaming. "Get out! Get out and hit the ground! We're being set up!"

Nick gets out and hits the ground as shots continue coming from three different positions. The street turns into a ghost town within seconds. Worst of all, Nick can't see a darn thing, and neither can the boys.

Bullets start striking the outside of the vehicle. Dave and Johnny fire back from the two sides of the large SUV. With his head down to the floor, Nick tries to crawl toward Charlie, but every time he moves, bullets miss him by inches. He finally makes one more attempt to get to the other side of the SUV and nearly gets shot in the head.

Dave screams, "Abandon the vehicle! Rocket attack is imminent!"

Nick looks at Charlie one more time and moves from the vehicle as fast as he can. The vehicle gets hit by a rocket and is tossed like a soda can. The vehicle bursts into flames, and the sky gets even darker from diesel fuel on fire.

Dave and Johnny are trying to figure out where the shots are coming from, but all they know is that it's more than one sniper shooting at them. Dave and Johnny try to back up, and they keep Nick behind them. After a fifteen-minute firefight, Johnny gets shot in the head. Dave tries to pull him away as he himself gets shot several times. No body armor will withstand the intensity of multiple rifle shots.

Nick is completely dumbfounded and trembling from the shock. His ears are ringing from the loud noises all around him. Sure, he was in the army, but it was in peacetime. As a matter of fact, this is his first real action, and he doesn't like it one bit. He can't believe what just happened. He doesn't know whether to cry, scream, run, or surrender to what's coming next. He is waiting to get shot.

Silence fills the air momentarily. A white Toyota pickup in the distance starts moving toward him. The pickup is carrying eight armed men. Nick thinks to himself, *I hope it's quick; I don't want to suffer for too long. I didn't know it was going to end like this.*

The pickup pulls right in front of him and slams on the brakes. A plume of dust hits Nick's face. A tall, skinny, heavy-bearded man gets out of the front seat, and the other men make a circle around Nick with their AK-47s pointed at his head. The tall, skinny man stands in front of Nick, staring at him with his intense brown eyes. The man looks as if he's wearing eye makeup. He is using the traditional antimony eye slave, one fine perfect line from one end of his eyelid to the other, going across just enough, making it look like he measured the dark line with a ruler. He commands Nick in Pashtu, "*Ra patssa, kapera!* [Get up, infidel!]"

Nick speaks fluent Pashtu and understands the tall man's command. Although he never imagined he would use his Pashtu skills in a situation like this, Nick puts his kidnapping training to use and understands to cooperate fully because the first few hours are the most critical, and one must cooperate and not resist.

The tall, dark, bearded man blindfolds Nick, ties his hands and legs together, and commands his men to throw him in the back of the pickup truck and drive before they have to confront someone from the coalition forces or the Afghan National Police (ANP).

Nick thinks, *All this firefight in the busy city, and I didn't see a single policeman in or around the area. What's their job, anyway, and where are they?*

Nick realizes Charlie's complaints about lack of loyalty are really true. Corruption will never encourage loyalty. As the American proverb states, "Easy come, easy go." It can't be truer of Nick's current situation and of the corrupt Afghan government.

The men chant, *"Alahuakber! Alahuakber!* [God is great!]" as they drive away from the scene.

CHAPTER THREE

Wishful Thinking

The pickup truck makes a series of turns, finally onto a dirt road. Nick can feel every bump. The men speak among themselves but offer no details about what they are going to do to him. Kidnapping an American in a broad daylight must be a gutsy thing to do. However, the men in the truck seem to be tense when they speak to each other.

The truck stops, and most of the men seem to leave, except at least two who are left with Nick. Nick has no idea where he is or what time it is. After what he guesses to be about twenty minutes, at least two men return and tell the men who are watching Nick to share the food and water they brought with the infidel.

"Remember, don't remove his blindfold."

The men untie Nick's hands but not his legs and tell him in Pashtu, "*Okhra* [Eat]."

"*Auba, auba* [Water, water]," Nick says.

The man puts a glass in Nick's hand, and Nick drinks the water up like there is no tomorrow. The man then hands him a bowl of something that's cold. Nick takes a sniff and knows it's yogurt. Then the man hands him what seems like flat, homemade bread. Nick asks, "*Kachogha?* [Spoon?]"

The two men break into loud laughter and reply, "*Lewanai* [crazy man] asks for spoon in the middle of nowhere."

Nick starts sipping the yogurt, takes a bite of the bread, and thinks, *I think this is what I'm going to be eating for a long time.*

One of the men returns and commands his men to untie Nick's legs. "We are changing the vehicle."

Nick is shoved in the back. The vehicle seems to have a backseat. Two men sit on each side of him. He hears both front doors shut simultaneously and assumes there are only four men riding with him this time.

The body odor of the men when the temperature is well above 120 Fahrenheit is overwhelming, and Nick has nowhere to turn or get away from it. The car starts moving. The windows come down, and Nick gets a little relief as the hot, dusty air enters the car.

The car drives through rough terrain, and by the way the gears are shifting, it sounds like they are going through some rugged mountains. The drive continues for over four hours, going up and down the grade. Finally Nick hears one of the men say, "We have to walk the rest of the way. We must walk around the military base to avoid checkpoints."

One of the men removes Nick's blindfold as nightfall nears. It must be around eight. Nick can smell cow dung burning in nearby homes. This is how Afghans bake their bread in clay ovens. The smell comforts him as he thinks of those who are living in those homes in the village. Nick wishes he lived in one instead of being dragged by the tall, skinny, bearded man and his troops.

After they walk for a couple of hours, some men come out of nowhere in the dark, with the skinny man showing absolutely no reaction.

I wonder who these men are, Nick thinks.

It seems the skinny man had planned it ahead of time and knows who these men are. Nick can't tell what they look like. The two men bring the skinny man two horses with supplies.

I think we're going to be walking for a few days, Nick thinks.

Nick realizes the skinny man has to avoid the military base and walk far from its security perimeter so as not to be detected. The skinny man and the two men who provided the supplies do not exchange many words. The two disappear into the darkness just as elusively as they appeared.

Nick is thirsty and exhausted. Finally, after walking for three hours, they make it to a bombed-out mud structure. The structure does not have a roof, but all four walls are still standing. On one of the walls, the *mihrab* indicates this building used to be a mosque.

Being in a desert, the nights get really cold. The skinny man says to his men, "We are going to spend the night here. We will leave before daybreak."

The skinny man brings Nick water from the supply on the back of the horse and hands him a piece of cornbread. No one really talks about anything, so Nick can't tell what the plan is. It must be around midnight, and the skinny man orders two of his men to stand guard and the rest to go to sleep.

It is really cold. Nick curls up and closes his eyes. It is dead silent except for the guards walking around. Sometimes they sit down. Nick thinks he is asleep, but in fact he is half asleep and totally aware. He dreams he is in New York on a cold, snowy day. He keeps walking around the city but cannot find any relief from the bitter cold. The dream goes on into the early morning hours when the skinny man kicks Nick on his buttocks. He wakes up right away and stands up in total disbelief over his real nightmare.

The journey continues right away, and Nick assumes it's because the skinny man wants to use the cool of the day in hopes of covering more ground early on. But there is no escape from the intense southern Afghanistan heat. The skinny man knows every water hole and stops from time to time to fill his American-made water container.

Nick's hands are tied behind him. He trips often since he is not used to rugged terrain. The skinny man orders one of his guards to tie Nick's hands in front of him so he can balance himself.

Hot weather peaks around noontime. The skinny man decides to take a rest and continue once sunset nears.

In the past, Nick wished to visit Afghanistan in peacetime to climb the mountains. *One thing this country has is its never-ending mountains,* Nick thinks. *It sure is the dreamland for tourists. But in the past thirty-five years, there are more mines than people in Afghanistan.* Nick's wish has come true but not how he imagined it.

Nick is exhausted. The skinny man and his troops climb these mountains in their sandals like goats. Finally, they stop, and Nick gets a good four hours of sleep and again is woken up by the skinny man, who tells him, "Eat something. We are going to walk all night long."

Nick is hungry but not for cornbread again. However, in the middle of the desert, this is what is available, and this is what he is going to eat. The darker the day gets, the more everything becomes freaky silent. Nick is so tired he wants the ordeal to end in whatever way possible. The caravan of four men and one hostage once more becomes mobile. There is no sound except that of horseshoes striking the sandy soil. There are flickers of light in the distance that appear and then disappear. These lights are from nearby police stations or bases of small coalition forces because Afghans don't have electricity in this part of Afghanistan.

Around what he guesses to be midnight, Nick starts to lag behind. His feet are swollen and full of blisters. This is his third day of wearing shoes around the clock. He is trying his best to keep up, but his legs are giving out. He is no longer able to keep up with the skinny man and his horses. Desperately, he edges closer to the second horse.

I can't keep up. If I fall behind, they'll probably shoot me in the head and leave me here to rot, Nick thinks. *I must keep up to survive. It will be over at some point. We will ultimately get there—wherever that is.*

Despite the danger of being kicked by the horse, Nick uses all of his energy to grab the animal's tail and hold on. Nick does not have the strength to walk on his own anymore, and the horse's tail pulls him along. The poor horse is also very tired and does not have the strength to kick.

Finally, the skinny man orders everyone to stop at the abandoned house in the middle of nowhere, appearing on the horizon as daybreak approaches. Most of the walls are missing, with only two rooms still usable. Both horses stop at the feeding area, which indicates these horses are veterans and know this place from their previous travels. The house has been without inhabitants since the Soviet invasion of the 1980s. Nick is very familiar with Afghan history. The Russians invaded Afghanistan in the late 1970s, and that lasted until 1988. The destruction from war with the Russians is still noticeable in many parts of Afghanistan. Pots and pans have been uniquely preserved and are still in their proper places. It seems the insurgents know the value of this house in the middle of nowhere and keep it in operating condition. The house is a good hiding place for the Taliban because the coalition forces do not suspect this location to be a hideout.

One of the skinny man's troops starts a fire right away. He runs to the horse and brings supplies to cook. The skinny man approaches Nick and hands him a hot cup of tea. Nick is beyond tired and takes a sip of the very hot, sweetened green tea. The tea works like a Tylenol, reaching his veins first and then his bones.

The skinny man orders all his men to take a good rest because this is the last day of their journey. To make sure Nick won't get any ideas, the skinny man chains him to the room's center beam.

The smell of lamb stew wakes up Nick. This is his fourth day without a hot meal. He is surprised, wondering where the skinny man got the meat in the middle of nowhere. Afghans eat dry lamb meat during the winter months and use it throughout the year because fresh meat is not available in nearby refrigerated markets—meaning that it does not exist.

Nick has had some really good meals in his days, but this one, after cornbread for four days, tastes like a meal from heaven. One of the men hands him a tall glass of tea to wash it down with. Nick has never appreciated a meal this much in his entire life.

Soon after the meal, the skinny man makes a phone call, and again they set off on their journey. It must be four in the afternoon. It's a hot and dusty day. Nick can barely walk as the fatigue really gets a hold of him. He is dragging himself and holds onto the horse's tail again.

It isn't more than a half hour since they left the abandoned house, and Nick hears helicopters in the distance. The sound makes the skinny man very nervous. He tells his men, "Do not panic; it will pass. If we run, they will come back, and God knows what will happen."

The helicopters get closer and closer. Nick hopes they will see him. *I think they know where I am. I think they're coming to rescue me,* he thinks. He is hallucinating at this point. Nick thinks somehow people magically know he was with Charlie and are now looking for him. Despair always creates a false hope.

The skinny man walks slowly and casually, pretending he sees nothing and hoping that they will not see him, either.

I think this is a good time for me to run or somehow wave so they can see me. I think I should do it, Nick thinks.

Nick is in a world of hallucinations when one of the helicopters detects the skinny man and his troops. One of the helicopters turns around while the second starts to make circles to create a security perimeter in case insurgents are hiding with their rocket launcher.

I think this is the perfect time for me to run! Nick thinks.

Nick is about to make his run when the helicopter shoots a warning shot. The skinny man orders everyone, "Stop, but do not run! If you run, they surely will shoot everyone. Stop and do nothing."

Nick is glad he didn't make a run for it. He would have been the first one to get shot. The helicopters apparently do not detect a threat and fly on to their intended destination. Every muscle in Nick's body is jumping from the frightening experience. For the first time, he sees fear in the skinny man's eyes, too. Nick has always loved seeing helicopters take off and land because they seem to be the most fantastic pieces of machinery in the sky. But he has never seen a helicopter in combat mode. They surely are the scariest pieces of machinery in the sky.

The skinny man thanks God that this frightening experience is over. Kidnapping an American would have been very difficult to explain, as Nick can clearly observe by his facial expressions. After two more hours of tiresome walking, they reach a village. The skinny man and his troops are welcomed by kids and elders. The kids eagerly look at the foreign man. Somehow, the news of the captured man arrived before the captured man did.

The skinny man tells his men, "*Dekharira worasdio* [By the grace of God, we have reached our final destination]." He orders his men to take the infidel to the dark room and close the double wooden doors as soon as possible. "Give him plenty of water so he doesn't die on us. All of our hard work would go to waste." The skinny man is born and resides here and is the commander of some two hundred men in the most isolated part of Uruzgan province. Nick notes how the villagers receive him. The dark room is a detached one-room, mud hut far from nearby homes.

The two men untie Nick's hands and start walking him to the dark room. The men tie him to a chain that is secured to the center pole of the room. Nick asks to relieve himself, and one of the men shows him a bucket not too far from where he is standing.

Nick slowly leans against the center pole, slides down, and sits in complete disbelief. Shaking his head and looking down at the floor, he says, "This is not exactly what I had planned. Charlie, what did you get me into? Who are these people? What do they want from me? Is this how it's going to end? What have I put my family through? I should have listened to Lisa when she told me to stay away from adventures."

For Nick, it is mostly all questions, and he can't come up with a single answer. He can hear people talking outside. Kids are trying to find a peephole anywhere on the wall so they can have a look at the infidel. They have never seen a foreigner up close except coalition troops going through their town in full gear. But this one is different, a foreign man all to themselves, and they want to know what a foreigner really looks like.

The two guards shove the kids away from the room. The skinny, bearded man warns the townspeople and kids as well. "Who we have here is nobody. You are not to say a word to anyone. If you do, I will personally cut your head off so your shoulders can feel lighter."

The tall, skinny man does not want word to spread. He must protect his prize with all of his power and not let anyone speak about or report this to anyone.

The townspeople immediately get the skinny man's message loud and clear, and the kids immediately move from the room and start running toward their homes. The night guard closes the double wooden doors.

The room gets really dark. The room was hot to begin with but gets even hotter when the door is shut. Nick tries to process the events of the past four days. He is clueless about what is going to happen next. He puts his head between his knees and starts to sob like a little baby. Somehow, crying does offer temporary relief. Nick thinks of the saying, "Men are harder than a rock and softer than a rose." At this moment, Nick is a man who is softer than a rose.

Every man has a breaking point, and for Nick, this is it. He watched hostage-taking videos and how to deal with it before all of his deployments, but no video will ever prepare a man for the real experience of being kidnapped.

Nick is being held against his will in an unknown place and among people he has nothing in common with. He has never in his entire life felt so lonely, nor has he ever felt so hopeless and helpless. Nick may still be in shock and not realize the seriousness of his situation, but he may in fact be held indefinitely or make a stupid mistake and be shot by tomorrow or be rescued by morning. These kinds of thoughts do not cross his confused mind at this stage of his captivity. All he can think about is his wife and children. He wishes he could somehow magically fly from this miserable dark room and fall into his family's arms.

The unfamiliar sounds and smells are driving him crazy. He doesn't hear or smell anything that he can relate to. If he could, this miserable journey might be easier to bear.

Tomorrow is a new day, Nick tells himself. *After every night, there is always a day. I will make it. Yes, I will. I am not going to let this get to me. Giving up will either kill me or turn me into a madman.*

Nick must accept his current situation and deal with it logically. Emotional decisions will get him killed.

CHAPTER FOUR

The Despair

Nick is scared, angry, sad, and confused above all.

Why me? he keeps asking himself over and over. *This was a two-hour trip, just like Charlie promised. No one was supposed to die. What went wrong? No one is looking for me. They don't even know I was with Charlie. What's going to happen now? Am I being held for ransom?*

And yes, indeed, things can go wrong fairly quickly here in Afghanistan, often without warning. There are no laws to be protected by, there are no agreements to be made, and the worst part is, human life is worth less than a sheep's or goat's life in this country. *When it comes to loyalty, there is none to speak of. Everyone with a rifle and any unemployed thug makes a commander. This is true on both sides, the Afghan government and the Taliban*, Nick thinks.

At this point, Nick is completely demobilized and demoralized. He is not able to stand or walk. For a city slicker like him, walking for four days has taken its toll. He will walk normally again once his body recovers, but it will take him a good month or so to be able to do that. Being tied to a center pole of the room will make the recovery even more difficult. However, he needs to move around using the room's length so he is once again able to walk normally.

Nick is going in and out of confusing thoughts when a man walks in with a dirty mattress in one hand and a pillow and blanket in the other. The mattress and pillow look as if they were used by a mechanic who never took a shower in his entire life—shiny and smelly. The man walks back out. The kids are eager to see the man captured by their village *mujahedeen* (freedom fighters). But the second man guarding the double wooden door will not allow the kids to come in or have a look at the captured man because the group fears the word may spread, prompting a coalition forces raid on the village.

The first man walks back in as Nick notices it's getting dark and nightfall is near. The man holds a bowl of food and a tall stainless steel cup of water. The man also brings him some old traditional Afghan clothing that has never seen ironing. He commands Nick to change and eat his food. The man stands close by to watch the captured man eat.

It takes Nick a good half hour to eat and change into the Afghan traditional clothes. The guard walks closer and puts the chain back on Nick's left hand. The chain has enough slack for him to move around. As Nick tries to sit down and make himself comfortable, the skinny, black-bearded man walks in. He orders the guard to bring him a chair. The guard quickly runs out and brings the skinny man a homemade bench to sit on. The skinny man sits down, looks at Nick, reaches into his vest pocket, and, still looking at Nick, pulls out a shiny, stainless steel can. He removes the cover, which has a mirror on the top, and reflects the light from a single kerosene light onto Nick's face. He then scratches the surface of the green Afghan dip *Naswaar*, picks up dip with the can cover, and skillfully shoots it under his tongue.

Voices can be deceiving, Nick thinks. He was so scared and confused in the course of his kidnapping and the sandstorm, he thought this man was very tall and well built. *This man is not large, nor is he tall,* thinks Nick. *He's not more than five foot four. But his eyes are sure scary.*

The skinny man composes himself, sits up straight, and asks Nick in Pashtu, "*Ta tarjuman yee?* [Are you an interpreter?]"

Nick tells him no.

The skinny man then introduces himself as Molawee Abdul Satar, commander of the Islamic Emirates of Afghanistan of greater Uruzgan province.

Nick is confused at this point as to why this person thinks the Taliban government still exists. "I thought Karzai was the president of Afghanistan," he says.

To Nick's surprise, the Taliban still think their government is the law of the land. Their communications are still written on former official letterhead with *Islamic Emirates of Afghanistan* in bold. Nick had seen many of these letters before circulating in the intelligence community.

Molawee Satar says to Nick in Pashtu, "You have dark hair and dark eyes. You are not an American. You are in fact a *terjuman*."

Nick again insists, "I am not an interpreter. I am a UN worker, and I am here to help the Afghan people."

Molawee again interrupts Nick and tells him, "We really hate *terjuman*. They serve as spies working for the Americans. We especially hate the ones who come from America. They have forgotten their ways of life and are here to make money with our blood. Most of them don't speak one language properly to communicate and get villagers killed for no reason. I really hate interpreters."

"Well, I'm a UN worker, not a *terjuman*," Nick insists.

"I didn't see a UN mark on your vehicle," Molawee says.

"I was with a friend out meeting someone," Nick says.

"Oh, the spy you are talking about. I took care of him before you showed up," Molawee says.

"I don't know of any spy. I wanted to see the city, that's all."

"Well, I don't like liars, and I don't like interpreters. If you are lying, that makes you an interpreter *and* a liar."

For Molawee Satar, the mission is accomplished, Nick realizes. What he wanted was to confirm that Nick is an American. Nick's life is worth a lot in a capital sense. An American government worker or someone working for an international organization is the most sought-after prize to capture, and an American interpreter is the second most sought-after prize in a monetary sense. Nick's capture gives Molawee great bargaining power with the coalition forces.

Nick doesn't say another word because any weakness from him will empower Molawee even more.

Molawee tells Nick, "This is not over. You will be seeing a lot of me."

Molawee mumbles to his men to allow some time for things to cool down, and they can take pictures and videos later. Molawee walks out.

Nick lies down on his dirty mattress. The guard shuts off the kerosene light, walks out, and padlocks the double wooden door behind him.

"My first night in captivity," Nick says to himself.

Exhaustion and constant fear keep him awake. He falls asleep sometime in the early morning. Around five o'clock in the morning, roosters crow, and not too long after that, the prayer call, *Azaan*, wakes Nick up. He has spent most of the night thinking about his family—if he will be fortunate enough to see them again or if this is the place he will die in. He can't read the situation. It's too early for him to tell what's going to happen to him. One thing that really bothers Nick is that no one knows he was with Charlie. In a situation like this, chances are no one will look for him.

Days pass, and there is no sign of Molawee Abdul Satar. Nick gets used to the routine of waking up, eating, exercising, and taking a peek through the single dirty window about five and a half feet above the floor, which serves as the only source of light during the day. His legs are getting stronger, and he is able to stand for longer periods of time.

Nick sometimes sees kids running around. Sheep and goats herded by small children and occasionally women go by. The women are wearing variously colored *burqas*—mustard, light blue, dark blue, dark green. They are following their spouses or grownup sons. Nick also hears helicopters fly overhead from time to time. In most kidnapping cases, the Taliban hold more than one person in one place, and therefore communication takes place. However, Nick is the only one being kept in this dark, isolated, detached room. He has no link to the outside world. For him, the only real connection is with the Taliban commander, Molawee Abdul Satar.

Back home, Bob, Nick's boss, does not know where to begin with his search. He is clueless about how to proceed or where the starting point should be. On top of that, Lisa is calling Bob nonstop. Bob has contacted just about every American agency, from the State Department to military people. He even contacted the Pakistani government agencies, but all of his efforts come back fruitless. Bob is confused about what happened to Nick. It is not like Nick to disappear like this. He does not fit the careless character type of some young and stupid kid.

Lisa keeps herself busy at all times for the sake of the children and for her sake. All she can do is hope for the best. It is devastating not knowing what happened to her husband. It is as though the ground split open and swallowed Nick. The hardest part is that she always has to come up with some creative story to tell the kids. They are still very young and buying whatever she tells them. But for how long? She spends most nights in the living room after the kids go to sleep, waiting for the phone to ring. The only thing that keeps her sane is hope. She hopes somehow Nick will walk in, and she will be right there in the living room to greet him. She has no idea what he is going through right about now or if he is even alive.

Nick is being held in an old, abandoned shop far from the main village. He can tell from the supply boxes littering the dirt floor and the shelves built on three different walls, which lack real workmanship. Most of the boxes have *Made in Pakistan* written on them.

It has been exactly forty-nine days since Nicholas Blake was first brought in and held in this shop. Now he has a fully grown beard. His hair almost reaches his shoulders and is lice infested. His fingernails are dirty and longer than they ever have been. In the past forty-nine days, he has not seen water except in the form of drinking water. The longest Nick can remember going without taking a shower was three days during his previous travels between Iraq or Afghanistan and the United States. The isolation is driving him mad.

The guard, who's been there all this time, comes in as usual, except this time he has a green plastic water pitcher, a bar of soap, and an old towel in his hand. He leaves the room and comes back with a razor blade. The guard approaches Nick and tells him in Pashtu, "I am going to shave your hair." The sharp, retractable razor blade does not look very assuring, as Nick has watched some very disturbing videos on YouTube in the past.

Nick asks, "Why?"

The guard tells Nick, "Because you look like an animal! Hold still. I am really good at this."

Nick gets his head shaved and asks the guard to shave his beard, too, but the guard tells him the beard stays. He hands Nick nail cutters and asks him to wash up and to use lots of soap "because you really stink!"

Nick does his best with the single water pitcher and washes up the best he can. He hears Molawee Satar's voice in the background and tells himself, *Something is up.*

Molawee Satar walks in with fifteen other men and tells everyone to settle down. Nick is anxious. He suspects Molawee's return must have a motive. Molawee's first question to Nick is, "Are you an interpreter?"

Nick replies, "No."

"Okay, I believe you," Molawee says.

"I am going to take some pictures and videos to send to your family," Molawee says.

Nick asks, "How do you know my family?"

"Well, I don't know your family, but there is something called the Internet. I can post your video, and someone will turn up and claim you. Now, here is what I am going to do. I am going to take some pictures, and then you are going to sit and eat, and I am going to take your videos."

There's no such thing as a free lunch, Nick thinks. *Molawee is up to something, but my video will be out, and there is a good chance someone will recognize me and people will start to look for me.* Nick at this point will try anything to get the word out. After all, publicity is good.

Nick agrees to Molawee's demands and starts posing as Molawee requested. When he's finished, Molawee's men set up a short table. They ask Nick to sit down cross-legged and then he will receive a meal. He sits down, and Molawee's men bring him a large meal consisting of brown rice with raisin, a typical Afghan dish, and a set of utensils. For the past forty-nine days, Nick has been eating with his dirty hands, food that one would feed their dogs, and this is a total surprise. He is videotaped while he eats.

After a grand meal, Nick is asked to read a statement condemning the US government and other coalition forces for invading Afghanistan, which the men will tape. Nick is reluctant at first, but he doesn't have much choice since armed men with rifles, long swords, and black masks pulled down over their faces are standing right behind him.

Photo sessions and videotaping become a ritual as weeks go by. The insurgents' demands become more and more aggressive. Sometimes they demand the release of hundreds of their men from jail, and sometimes they demand cash. Molawee Satar gains fame and fortune from Nick's unfortunate ordeal. The coalition forces continuously pay through many channels, and ultimately Molawee Satar benefits from the ISAF cash flow through different channels. The coalition forces are hoping to get some kind of information so they can start looking for Nick. However, Molawee Satar is a very clever man. He does not deal directly with the coalition force and creates confusing channels to stop any leads that would ultimately lead to him and his network. With the blessing of the Inter-Services Intelligence (ISI), he should be safe and sound for as long as he is able to keep the movers and shakers of the ISI happy.

CHAPTER FIVE

The Hallucination

As time goes on, Molawee Abdul Satar grows more and more impatient because most of his demands are not being met the way he hoped for. He starts threatening to kill Nick if his demands are left unanswered. *Nothing I can do*, Nick tells himself. *This is hopeless. How long are they going to keep me here? Is there a trial? Or am I being held without any reason?*

Nick realizes Molawee's intent. He understands the roots of his ignorance, which leave Afghanistan in great danger of splitting again. Nick has a very good understanding of Afghan history. He knows he is being used by Molawee Satar. He also realizes that in reality, the Taliban in general have become more entrepreneurial. The goodwill that existed in the early years of their struggle has diminished altogether. In the late 1990s, the US government invited the Taliban leadership to meet in Washington so the Taliban could become a mainstream form of government that would be accepted by the rest of the world.

However, the Taliban evolved from a goodwill government saving Afghanistan to their true selves as Pakistani ISI (Pakistan's intelligence agency) servants and puppets. The Taliban are taking orders directly from the Pakistani intelligence agency as well as the Pakistani government, assuming the rest of Afghanistan will become the next Pakistani province like the rest of the northwestern frontier. *What a trick world politics is*, Nick thinks.

Meanwhile in New York, Bob Welch—Nick's boss—is trying to put the pieces of the puzzle together and figure out what has really happened.

33

Bob receives phone calls from Lisa, Nick's wife, on a daily basis. Bob assures Lisa that he is doing his best to resolve the situation and find a solution with the State Department and that he is in contact with them every day. He tells Lisa the photos and videos he receives show Nick in good health and in a good mental state. Lisa tries to watch some of the videos circulating on the Internet, but she wants to remember her husband the way he left, not in despair, because it would be difficult for her to bear.

Molawee Abdul Satar so far has had ten of his men released from jail and sees opportunities to have more of his demands met, so he tries to keep Nick for as long as possible. However, at the same time, the tribal elders are growing weary and are starting to question Molawee's motives. The villagers of the area know that Nick's captivity poses a great danger to their villages. No Afghan family ever wants the humiliation associated with night raids, which broadens the hard feelings between the Afghans and the coalition forces. Children are terrorized by night raids, and in most instances, innocent women and children are killed for no reason.

The question that the village people are asking is, "How does a night raid build bridges or win hearts and minds?" The twelve-year-old US invasion of Afghanistan has proven to be ineffective at best. That is why the village elders want a solution to this problem now, before it's too late. With the passage of time, the village elders are becoming more and more frustrated with Molawee. They want an end to his reckless behavior.

The village elders call a *shura* (meeting) and invite elders from five different villages. They invite Molawee Abdul Satar as well. The *shura* is held after dark because the elders fear detection from coalition forces. Most gatherings are treated as Taliban meetings, and many weddings are turned into funerals, which also prompt bombings by coalition forces, resulting in more funerals. The cycle continues.

The *shura* consists of fifteen elders from five different regions and three different tribes. The *shura* begins with a prayer by the most prominent tribal elder, Haji Mohamed Qader. The meeting commences with side stories, discussion of water rights, and other matters of local importance, followed by a dinner of rice and lamb stew with a mixed tomato and onion salad.

After dinner, the *shura* members stop talking and focus on why the meeting was called. First, Haji Mohamed Qader, the most respected *shura* member, reminds everyone of the Pashtun culture and way of living. Respect above all is what the Pashtun culture is about. Haji Qader reads each and every code of honor, not that the *shura* members don't know what these codes are, but to make a statement and to intensify his point of view.

"*Melmastia* [Hospitality] means showing profound respect to those visiting a Pashtun home. A Pashtun will offer anything and everything he has to keep his guest feeling welcome in his home.

"*Nanawatai* [Asylum] means a Pashtun will let anyone stay at his or her home if someone seeks asylum, regardless of the crime committed or other reasons, and regardless of race, religion, and nationality, until the person's problems are resolved in a civilized manner.

"*Badel* [Justice/Revenge] means to seek justice or revenge against those who have done wrong, such as insult, murder, or rape.

"*Tureh* [Bravery] means that a Pashtun will defend his country, land, family, and women at all costs, even with his or her own life.

"*Wafadari* [Loyalty] means that loyalty must be paid to one's tribe first. Next come family, neighbors, and friends.

"*Imandari* [Righteousness] means that a Pashtun must always think well, speak well, do good deeds, behave respectfully, and respect elders, both men and women.

"*Isteqamat* [Belief in God] means that all men are created equal, that no one is better than the other. There is only one God that a Pashtun trusts in.

"*Ghayrat* [Self-Honor and Dignity] means that a Pashtun must first respect himself, and then respect for others will come automatically. Respect begins at home and spreads outward to the rest of the society.

"*Namus* [Honor of Women] means that Pashtuns will defend the honor of their women selflessly. Pashtuns will protect women at all costs from physical harm, indignity, and humiliation.

"I, Haji Mohamed Qader, want to remind everyone that the Pashtun culture and way of living have existed for thousands of years. We may have our differences with other tribes, but the end result and our way of living have always been built on respect—respect for elders, which results in serving the best interests of each and every one of us. We have dealt with thirty-five years of war. Our country and our people have been through a lot of hardship. But all of these changes must not change the way we live or make us forget our codes of honor."

Powerful words indeed by Haji Qader. However, village people know that none of the honor codes have been practiced by most Pashtuns in the past thirty-five years of war and infighting.

Each member of the *shura* nods his head in agreement with Haji Qader, except Molawee Abdul Satar. He looks as if every word from Haji Mohamed Qader has struck him like a bullet, and he shakes his head in complete disagreement.

Molawee drops into the conversation, without being permitted to speak, and says, "Our old way of living does not work for what we are facing now. The enemy has changed, and our Islamic teachings tell us to declare war against the infidels."

Haji Qader once again reminds Molawee, "Pashtun's ways of living will never change. What you are doing is dangerous, and you are attracting unwanted attention to our community. You are putting our villages in danger of night raids. We have lost four generations of youngsters, the future of this country. This kind of dangerous thinking has to stop. We may have more than forty countries fighting here, but the real danger is from our neighbors—one neighbor to the west and the other to the south. Pakistan will disrupt peace in Afghanistan at all costs. They don't want a strong, educated Afghanistan. They want Pashtuns to stay ignorant and for them to never bring up the Durand Line in political conversation, which has been expired for years now."

Haji Qader is an educated person and goes on to shed some light on the past history. "The Durand Line was formed by the British in 1893 by Mortimer Durand before the formation of current Pakistan to separate Pashtun tribes of the south from the north, which has expired in the 1990s. In a way, this imaginary line has proven to make the Pashtuns less powerful and the British's divide-and-conquer policy successful. The divide-and-conquer political ideology of the British government in the past has created many political problems all over the world. The consequences and failures of this ideology are far greater now than what the British thought at the time. One that is most significant is the Durand Line leaving a buffer between Afghanistan and modern Pakistan, which is the breeding ground for terrorism and fundamentalism. Pakistan under no condition ever wants the Durand Line conversation to come up, and, Molawee Satar, you have been created by the Pakistani ISI to stop the expiration of the 1893 agreement between Afghanistan and the British. Do you realize this, Molawee?"

To call Pakistan an archenemy is to accuse Molawee Satar of being a Pakistani agent, as most Afghans now believe Pakistan's ill intentions are brought about by tapping into Afghans' ignorance. Molawee gets up and leaves in protest. Disappointed, Haji Qader calls off the *shura* because he and other members fear a negative reaction from Molawee Abdul Satar against different tribe members. The inconclusive meeting reminds Haji Qader of the inconclusiveness and indifference of Afghan people as a whole.

"The disappointment lingers on, and precious lives are lost every day, but we can't leave our ignorance behind," Haji Qader mumbles to himself.

Nick has been living in a closed shop for the past six months and knows very well that his cooperation has led to Molawee's success in using the situation to his full advantage. Nick tells himself, *I have to do something. I have to get out of here, and I never will if the coalition forces keep cooperating with Molawee.*

Nick is thinking of escape. *But how?* he asks himself. *I don't even know where I am, and even if I get away, I won't get too far before Molawee's men capture me or kill me.*

He notices the day guard, Noor Agha, is getting sloppy with his security procedures, but the night guard, Hakimullah, is still very watchful. Nick tells himself, *It's very dangerous, but I have to get away during the day, and it has to be when Noor Agha takes his afternoon nap. But which way should I run?*

Nick remembers the Pashtuns' *Pashtunwali* honor codes. He keeps repeating to himself, *Nanawatai, nanawatai … asylum!* He repeats each code in his head to find a map, to build a system as a road map to freedom. He remembers so many stories about Pashtun codes from history books. The past few long days have finally brought him some hope.

Nick keeps telling himself, Nanawatai *is my way out. Yes,* nanawatai. *If I can get out of here, I will knock on the first door and call, 'Nanawatai!' If I can only make it to the first door … if I can only make it to the first door!*

37

Nick starts monitoring Noor Agha's routines. *I will watch him for the next few days, study his behavior, and note his weak points. I will do my best not to be noticed.*

Nick saves small amounts of grease from his food in a plastic bag and hides it. He will use it to make his hand slippery so he can slip it free of the chain's ring when his escape plan comes together.

The next day, on a cold January morning when the temperature has dipped below freezing at night, the thick mud walls of the room have kept the temperature around sixty-five degrees. The single window is allowing the sun to enter the room and warm it. Nick stares at the window facing east and witnesses the sunrise. He can tell it's about six, and the guard is about to change.

Nick again goes over all the steps of his escape plan. At the same time, he tries to refine every step and adds new ideas to each because he knows too well that his first failure will be his last, and he will pay with his life. Nick also realizes that in order to gain the day guard Noor's trust, he should be friendlier to him. This way, Nick can play the friend card and use Noor for his grand plan. For Nick, diplomacy comes naturally. After all, he is a diplomat by profession.

What Nick doesn't realize is that Molawee Abdul Satar has his own grand plans. Molawee has planned to make his last propaganda videotape in which he is going to convert Nick to Islam and show the world that Nick has willingly agreed to the idea and that it was his captive's idea to make the tape. What Molawee will try to show is that Nick himself has realized in the past ten months of captivity that he has been blind all his life and has missed the opportunity to experience the great religion of Islam.

Molawee Satar's constant request for a large ransom has been denied by his Western contacts. In frustration, Molawee has made a deal with the Al-Qaida in Pakistan to transfer Nick to them in exchange for a large amount of cash. Pakistan's ISI has made it possible for Molawee to strike such a deal. For Molawee, this is the deal of a lifetime—to get paid from two different parties, the ISI and the Al-Qaida in Pakistan.

For Molawee, this one hostage alone has brought him fame, fortune, and prestige among terrorist groups, and this last deal will make him set for life. If things get hot in Uruzgan, Molawee can always depend on his

ISI contacts on the other side of the border, and he will be welcomed by the ISI with open arms.

Nick has gone through his plan many times when he hears Molawee Satar's voice telling Noor Agha, the day guard, to prepare Nick for his last video session. Nick gets nervous and asks himself, *What does he mean by last session? Is he going to kill me afterwards? I really need to get out of here before it's too late.*

Once again, Noor Agha walks in through the gate with a large bucket of water, a pitcher, a new bar of soap, and a new pair of *shalwar kamis,* Afghan traditional clothing. In an unusual move, Noor Agha approaches Nick with a smile and tells him, "I brought you lots of water so you can wash yourself."

Nick asks, "Why?"

Noor Agha replies, "You have no idea how bad you stink! I can smell you all the way outside the gate."

Nick remembers the day he was first kidnapped when he sat between the two men inside the car. He remembers how bad they smelled, and now he tells himself, *The tables have turned. I can't even smell myself.*

"Make sure to wash up in that corner." Noor Agha points to a small concrete patch not more than one meter by one meter with a drain. "Don't make a mess inside the room and take as long as you want."

Noor takes the chain off of Nick's hand and displays his pistol to let Nick know who is in charge, warning him not to get any ideas. He then walks out of the gate.

Nick touches the water. It's warm, just the right amount. Nick hasn't seen this much water in ten months. He takes his clothes off, including his underwear that he has been wearing for the past ten months. He picks up the pitcher full of water and slowly tilts it over his head. He fills the pitcher again from the bucket and this time throws the water all over his body while he is sitting down. He picks up the soap and washes. Starting with his short hair and very long beard, he washes and washes and tells himself, *Such a little thing that I took for granted. A full body wash after ten months. It's so great.*

Nick stands up, picks up the bucket with less than half of the water left, and empties it over his head. He holds his head up, and water enters his nostrils. He feels the sensation of drowning, the kind of sensation one gets swimming in a pool when breathing incorrectly.

Nick picks up the small towel Noor brought him. He tries his best to dry himself. He picks up his newly sewed clothes. He takes a whiff of the new fabric and thinks, *I wonder what the occasion is.*

He puts on his new, dark navy clothes and calls to Noor that he is done. Noor walks in, and Nick asks him, "What do you want to do with the old clothes?"

Noor tells him, "You will find out in a minute." Noor then asks Nick to put his old clothes into a plastic bag and hand them to him. Noor walks out of the gate, leaves the gate open, pulls a lighter out of his pocket, and sets fire to the plastic bag.

Nick smiles at Noor and tells himself, *I think they really deserved that!*

Noor forgets to lock the gate, and Nick gets a chance to peek outside. He looks around and locates some homes in the distance within less than a half mile. Nick then wonders what Molawee Satar's next move is and what he is going to ask him tonight.

Noor walks in and brings Nick his lunch. He puts the chain back on Nick's hand and walks out quickly, locking the gate behind him. Nick slowly pulls out his grease bag, picks the grease off the top of the food, puts it in the bag, and closes it.

I think I have enough grease to take the chain off of my hand, he thinks.

CHAPTER SIX

The Grand Escape

The short winter days bring Molawee Satar in earlier than usual. He sits across from Nick with a fake smile on his face. Molawee opens up the conversation by saying, "You know how lucky you are? You are going to be released to your government in five days, and I think you have been the most patient man I have ever seen."

Nick puts on his diplomatic face and replies, "I really appreciate your hospitality, and I hope I have been a good guest."

Molawee quickly changes the subject and tells Nick, "Before I release you and since I have been a good host, I need to make a last video. I know you, as a Westerner, must have studied my great religion."

Nick replies, "Yes, I studied Islam in school."

Molawee tells Nick, "In order for me to release you, you have to convert to Islam."

Nick, in total confusion and surprise, asks, "Why?"

Molawee says, "I think it's important for the world to know that my religion is a peaceful one."

Nick puts his head down and thinks to himself, *Indeed a peaceful religion, but what version of Islam are you practicing?* Nick looks back at Molawee and tells him, "This is really too much to ask of a man."

Molawee, with his tricky style, tells Nick, "But don't you want to be with your wife and children? They must miss you a lot, and I am sure you also miss them a lot."

Nick at this point wants to believe anything. He can for a brief moment feel the warmth of Lisa's hand, smell her, and feel her presence. He can hear the voices of his children. Nick asks Molawee, "You are going to release me after I convert?"

Molawee says, "Well, of course. You have my word."

Nick, distrusting his captor, agrees to Molawee's condition and tells himself, *It will buy me five more days. I really have to get out of this place now.*

Later that evening, Molawee Satar comes in with his men and his video camera. One of his men fires up a generator, and the room lights up. Nick hasn't seen lights this bright in months. The last time he witnessed such bright lights was in the transit tent at KAF (Kandahar Airfield).

Molawee prepares a statement for Nick to read and hands it to him. "Read this a couple of times. You are going to read it out loud once we are done converting you."

Molawee leads a prayer as his man videotapes the entire conversion session. Nick reads the statement carefully prepared by Molawee. Soon after, Nick pours his heart out as he reads the statement. The statement is mostly coded verses of Molawee's personal intentions and what he can gain from kidnapping. The statement is versed toward the coalition forces to let them know what he wants in the near future. Molawee gives a signal to his men to stop taping once Nick is done reading.

Nick asks Molawee, "How was it?"

Molawee looks at him for a brief moment and walks out of the room without saying a word. Nick realizes what has just happened here. Molawee has just gotten what he wanted. Nick sarcastically shouts in English to Molawee, "Mission accomplished!"

Nick now knows that Molawee Satar will never release him. It was just a last grand show for him, and Nick has no idea what is going to happen to him. One thing Nick is sure of—he will never be released, and he should move on to his own plan to get away from Molawee and his men.

The lights are shut off, and total darkness once again surrounds the abandoned shop. Nick is sure that whatever Molawee's next plan is, it will be much worse than what he has been through the past ten months. One thing Nick is also sure of—he has five days before Molawee moves him to a totally unknown place. Nick lies down on his dirty mattress and falls into deep thought. Another thing Nick is aware of—despair will not help him. What this situation needs is action.

What do I have to do to gain Noor Agha's trust? Nick thinks. *Five days is a very short time to make someone trust you, but I have to do it no matter how dangerous it is. This is my one and only chance to get out of this place. I know that whatever happens is worth the risk.*

The next morning, Nick wakes up tired because he has been nervous all night. He again starts planning. *My first move is to somehow convince Noor to leave the gate open.*

Noor Agha walks in at seven o'clock in the morning and brings Nick his breakfast. With a smile, Nick thanks Noor and asks him, "Did you sleep well?"

"Yes," Noor replies.

"Thanks for breakfast."

"Okay. You have good day." Noor walks out with a silly smile on his face.

In the next five hours, Nick tries to come up with a good reason to ask Noor to leave the gate open. At noon, Noor brings Nick lunch and starts walking back out as usual. Nick calls him back and says, "Noor, listen."

Noor turns back and asks, "What is it?"

"Do you remember you said how bad this place smelled?"

Noor replies, "It still does!"

"I have an idea for how to make the smell go away," Nick says.

"How?" Noor asks.

"You can leave the gate open when you're sitting outside, maybe for a couple of hours." Noor seems to be thinking for a moment. "I've really noticed the smell since I washed myself, and I can imagine how bad it is for you to deal with day in and day out."

Noor looks at him and says, "I don't know."

Nick shows him his chain. "Look, I'm not going anywhere."

"Well, the smell is really bad, I have to agree. Okay, I will leave the gate open when I am on duty, but you are not going to tell the night guard."

"No, I won't do that," Nick says. *This is good*, Nick thinks. *For the next two days, I have to be on my best behavior so he doesn't suspect anything. And I have to get out on the third day because anything can change if I wait for the fifth day to arrive.*

43

Despite the anxiety he feels, Nick stays cool for the next two days and acts normal as Noor walks in and out of the room. After two days, Nick tells Noor, "I told you the room would smell better."

"Yes, it does," Noor agrees with a smile.

On the third day, Nick wakes up before dawn, nervous and scared. He tells himself, *Today is the day!*

For some reason, the night guard walks in and brings Nick his breakfast.

Nick asks, "Where is Noor?"

The night guard disregards Nick's question, walks out, and locks the gate behind him.

In total disbelief, Nick says to himself, *Oh no. This can't be happening. This wasn't part of the plan. What am I going to do now? I can't believe this. Of all days, Noor disappears now. How unlucky can I be? There'd better be a good explanation for this. Why now?*

Nick spends the entire day and night and into the next morning tossing and turning. He's about to lose his mind. *My plan, my plan. Everything changed just from a change of guard. I'm so stupid. I should have had a plan B, but it's too late now. I don't know what Molawee is going to do to me. I have only two more days before Molawee sends me wherever he's sending me.*

This morning is unusually cold, more than other nights. The cold, gusty winds were blowing all night long, and the padlock touching the wooden door makes a whistling sound. Nick is curled up in his blanket, with his head covered. The top of his blanket is covered with ice crystals from the moisture of his breathing. The cold is attacking him from two directions—from the bottom because of his thin mattress and from the cold in general. Nick hasn't slept. He doesn't even feel the bitter cold. He is numb from the failure of his plan.

He hears the gate open. *The devil is back,* Nick thinks.

He hears the breakfast tray dropped by his mattress. Nick is so disappointed he doesn't have the energy to remove the blanket from his face.

"Infidel, wake up!" Nick doesn't move. "Infidel, wake up! I brought you breakfast."

"Noor! Is that you?"

"Who else? I feel like I am married to you," Noor jokingly comments.

Nick jumps up from his bed and laughs like a madman. Noor says, "What has gotten into you? You're acting crazy."

"Oh, nothing. I was dreaming. I had a bad dream. I'm just glad I'm awake now."

"Okay. I brought you a jacket. It's really cold outside. Do you still want the gate open?"

"Oh yes, definitely. I don't feel cold. I'm just fine. By the way, where were you yesterday?"

"Oh, I went to the big bazaar to buy a phone card for my phone."

"Oh, I was just wondering what had happened to you. And thanks for breakfast."

"Okay, crazy man," Noor says as he walks out.

Nick gets up and tries to compose himself. He starts going through his plan over and over. At lunchtime, Noor brings him a tray of food and drops it in front of him. He heaves a sigh of relief and tells Nick, "You will be gone in two days, and I will have a chance to see my family again."

"That's a good thing," Nick says.

"Yes, of course. I feel like I have been in prison with you. I have never been on this kind of assignment before. I am always on top of the mountain, free."

Nick says, "I have never been on this kind of assignment, either!" Nick and Noor both laugh.

Nick doesn't feel like eating. *It's noontime,* he thinks. *Noor is going to pray, and around one thirty, he is going to take a nap. I have to be patient for the next hour and a half. Very patient.*

Nick is tempted to pull the grease from under the mattress and free his hand. *What if it takes too long to get the chain off? What if my hand doesn't come out? But patience—I have to wait despite the amount of anxiety I feel in the pit of my stomach.*

Nick patiently waits an hour and a half. It seems like months. Nick slowly picks up the chain without making a sound and walks toward the gate. He looks to the right and then to the left. Noor is leaning on the wall in the warm winter sun. His head is turned to the left with his *Balochistani* hat pulled down over his face.

He's asleep—I hope, Nick thinks.

Nick slowly walks back toward his mattress, quickly pulls out the grease bag, and picks out some grease with an old rag, trying not to get both of his hands slippery since only his left hand is attached to the chain. He then starts rubbing grease over his left hand with his right hand, which is attached to the chain. He grabs the corner of his blanket and starts pulling on the ring. His hand is too big, but that doesn't stop him from trying. He pulls hard. Sweat trickles down his forehead even though it's around sixty degrees inside the room. On the third try, he manages to pull the ring halfway down onto his hand. He pulls really hard this time and hears a crack in his upper thumb, but he is so nervous and scared he doesn't feel any pain. On the fourth try, he manages to free his hand, and the chain makes a loud noise.

Nick pretends to be asleep on top of the chain's ring momentarily, but Noor doesn't seem to have heard the chain. Nick gets out of the bed and slowly walks toward the gate. Noor is asleep. Nick looks around and sees no activity because most Afghans take a nap after lunch, right after the afternoon prayer.

He looks at the same homes he has looked at through the gate before and thinks, *Which one?* He locates a dry stream not more than four feet deep and tells himself, *I should walk through the dry bed, and if someone sees me, I can hide.*

Nick starts walking, and still no one is around. He walks some more and often ducks for a moment to avoid detection. He looks back at the abandoned shop one more time. Noor is still asleep.

Nick has already walked more than half the distance to the nearby homes. He tells himself, *I'm very close, and I hope the man of the house is home to open the door. If I knock on the wrong door, and the man of the house isn't home, I'm truly doomed.*

Nick keeps walking and hopes he finds the right door. He starts praying. *God, I haven't been calling on you as often as I should, but please get me through this one. Please, God, please.* Nick walks and prays at the same time.

Suddenly, a group of children run out of the nearby mosque as children do, and they see Nick walking in the dry bed. Complete silence surrounds the area for a moment, and then the children scream in unison, "The infidel! The infidel! He is getting away!"

Nick has no choice but to run as fast as he can. The children's screams wake up Noor and many neighbors. Noor starts running toward the homes and shouts, "Don't let him get away!" He starts shooting at the same time.

Nick is so scared and disoriented, his legs start to wobble. He is so close to the houses. "I have to make it! I have to make it to the first home!"

Noor is gaining on him and shooting single shots. Nick looks at five compounds—all really huge—and picks the biggest one because he assumes it belongs to someone prominent, a man with power. As Nick gets closer to the house, not more than ten meters away, Noor closes in. He aims at Nick's leg to prevent him from knocking on the door and shoots.

Nick drops immediately. He curls up in pain but doesn't give up. He starts crawling and makes it to the large, wooden door. Noor is still shooting, but he himself is scared of the consequences if Nick gets away and misses every shot.

Nick picks up a rock as he crawls to the door and uses it to knock as hard as he can. Nick shouts, "*Nanawatai! Nanawatai!* [Asylum! Asylum!]" He pounds on the large, wooden double door while Noor fires at him.

After constant pounding on the door, one side opens. Nick shouts, "*Nanawati! Nanawatai! Nanawatai!*" Suddenly, the gunfire stops, and Noor sees a man inside the open door. The man raises his hand and tells Noor it is over. Nick has been accepted as a guest in his home. Noor does not have a chance to fire again because the door has opened, which signals an automatic truce between the pursuer and the person seeking asylum. Noor puts his hands on his head in total disbelief and sits on the ground as the man pulls Nick into his home.

The man closes the gate, introduces himself as Gulbaz, and tells Nick, "I accept your plea for *nanawatai*. You are safe now, but getting out of here will be next to impossible. Molawee Satar is the king around this area, and his men are spread out over a large area. But for now, let's not think about that. Let me take care of your wound and clean you up. And welcome to a Pashtun home. No one can touch you. I will defend you with the last drop of my blood."

Nick is going in and out of consciousness, but he knows he is in good hands. He feels he is the luckiest man alive to have knocked on the right door.

CHAPTER SEVEN

Nanawatai

Gulbaz runs into the house, grabs a white cotton cloth and a can of brake fluid, and runs back toward Nick. Gulbaz asks Nick to lean back on the wall and let him look at his wound. He tells Nick, "Oh, you have been hit in your lower thigh, but there's an exit wound. Nothing to worry about. The cold weather will help the wound heal really fast. You will be on your feet in no time."

Gulbaz grabs the brake fluid and pours it on Nick's thigh. Nick feels the burn on his leg but doesn't make a sound. The brake fluid helps stop the bleeding. Gulbaz burns a ball of cotton and places it directly on both the entrance and exit wounds. Gulbaz wraps the white cotton around Nick's wounds and tells him, "This should take care of it."

Nick relaxes. He feels the pain in his left hand from when he removed the ring and tells Gulbaz, "I think I dislocated my thumb when I tried to remove the ring from my hand."

Gulbaz takes a look at his hand. He pushes Nick's finger joints around. Nick feels the pain in the upper part of his thumb. Gulbaz rubs it with both his hands until he hears it click. He tells Nick, "It is back in. I am going to wrap it with this cotton fabric. Make sure not to move your hand for a few days."

Nick is amazed by the remedies Gulbaz has used. Ordinary household items can stop bleeding and save a life. Nick was lucky to be injured in winter when the chance of a wound healing is much greater. If it had been during the hot summer months when temperatures climb well above 120 degrees, his chances of healing would have been below 10 percent, and infection would have been likely.

Nick is still recovering from the shock he has just gone through. At this point in his life, it is all about survival. A gunshot wound would have been a big deal if he had gotten it in New York. However, in Afghanistan, it is a daily occurrence for someone to get shot, blown up, or hit by a stray bullet.

Nick speaks really fast and feels dizzy from blood loss. The excitement he feels at this moment forces him to ask irrelevant questions. Although he has been accepted by Gulbaz into his home, Nick does not know how to behave or what the proper questions are.

Nick asks Gulbaz, "Where did you learn how to treat wounds?"

Gulbaz smiles and tells him, "We have no hospitals here, so treating wounds and fixing fractures is passed on from generation to generation. We can do the basic treatments, but bigger wounds and diseases are completely in the hands of God!"

Gulbaz tells Nick to hop onto his back so he can take him to the guesthouse, which is separate from the main house. Nick is embarrassed to hop onto an old man's back and tells Gulbaz he can try to walk himself. Gulbaz tells him, "First, I don't want you to put pressure on your leg because it will start bleeding again, and second, I may be old, but I can pick two of you up with no problem."

Nick hops onto the old man's back, and Gulbaz brings him into the guestroom.

Nick looks around the room. It's huge and very clean. The room smells like dust because of the dirt floors and mud walls. The floors are completely covered with Afghan carpets. There is no furniture but lots of *toshakona*, Afghan-style furniture that looks like mattresses laid around the room and designed to sit at floor level. It has bright, flowery designs. There are lots of large pillows against the walls for guests to lean on and sit cross-legged.

There are no pictures on the walls. The only picture he sees is a Mecca tapestry imprinted on a one-by-two, machine-made rug. There are lots of hand fans for guests to cool themselves on hot summer days. The guesthouse has a direct entrance from the outside also. Three small windows are tilted upward, allowing light to come in but keeping the sun from directly entering the room.

Gulbaz tells Nick, "I will bring you a blanket to keep you warm. You get some rest before dinner. I am going to see if I can find you something for pain."

Gulbaz walks to the corner of the room and opens a big knot on a large cloth covering a pile of blankets and pillows, *rakhtekhaw.* He pulls out a new blanket and hands it to Nick, telling him, "I will be back at dinnertime. I am busy with clearing the streams to my plantation because spring is on its way. You are safe here in my home. I will share with you what I eat. You keep your end of the bargain. All you have to do is respect my home and know your place and status."

Nick knows what he means because he is well aware of Afghan culture. He is a guest in this house and needs to respect the Afghan culture and way of living. Nick thanks him, and Gulbaz walks out of the room.

Nick has learned to speak Pashtu very well during his ten months of captivity. Gulbaz doesn't treat him like a foreigner, nor does Gulbaz feel as if a total stranger has just entered his life and home. Nick is a foreigner who has traveled from far, far away, and there are absolutely no commonalities between the two men to be shared, yet both live under the same roof, at least for now. What the future holds for both, no one knows.

Nick is amazed by Pashtun honor codes and often wonders how people with such strong social codes are unable to resolve the long and bitter feelings against each other. Is it the tribalism? He knows tribalism is one of the main causes behind the thirty-five-year-old war, as well as the lack of education caused by continuous war and the never-ending invasions by foreign forces that occur every fifty to one hundred years and wipe out all the achievements made within that period.

Afghanistan is cursed with strategic importance and tribalism, which has forced it to lose more than half the country to the Durand Line. It is in danger of losing its identity and being shared among its greedy, ill-intentioned neighbors, Nick thinks.

Over the next month, Nick regains his strength and is able to walk around the room, but he is eager to go outside and smell the spring air. Gulbaz is more and more busy, working on his plantation, and Nick wants to go out and help him. On the other hand, Nick is also aware of cultural sensitivities, and he does not want to put Gulbaz on the spot or impose his own wants and needs.

A total stranger walking around the house would be an insult to Gulbaz, and Nick is very well aware there might be women in this household. Nick sees that Gulbaz minds his own business and tries his best to make Nick feel comfortable. He does not want to ask Nick awkward questions or embarrass him in any way.

One evening, Gulbaz comes in carrying dinner and sits down. He looks very tired. Gulbaz always eats breakfast, lunch, and dinner with Nick, as tradition dictates. But tonight, Nick gets the feeling that Gulbaz wants to say more and wants to know more about Nick.

Gulbaz asks Nick if he is married. Nick says, "Yes, I am, and I have one boy and a girl."

Gulbaz says, "I, too, have a boy and a girl. My wife passed away when my boy was born, and he was born blind."

Nick says, "You didn't remarry?"

"No, I don't want my children to be ordered around by a stepmother. You married only one woman?"

Nick smiles and says, "Yes, only one time."

"But why?"

"Well, in my country, you are not allowed to marry more than one woman."

"Who doesn't let you marry more than one?"

"The government."

Gulbaz doesn't comprehend the concept of the government not allowing men to marry more than one woman. In frustration, he tells Nick, "I am going to work early in the morning, and if you feel better, you can come and help me."

Nick says, "I really want to help you."

Nick has been waiting for this moment, to be free a little, at least. Being caged up for a month in a room with absolutely no entertainment has been unbearable. However, he still prefers this room and being lonely over his ordeal with Molawee and his gang in an abandoned shop. The reminder of his captivity sends a chill through Nick's body every time he thinks about it, especially his grand escape.

The next day, on a crisp, cool March morning, Nick wakes up and is excited to go outside.

Gulbaz walks in, hands Nick a pair of sandals, and tells him, "Do you know you walked barefoot from Molawee Satar's place?"

Nick says, "No, I don't remember."

"Well, here is a pair of sandals. I hope they fit. And put this hat on because men don't walk around without a hat."

Nick walks out. The sun is about to rise, and he is surprised at how big the compound is. He turns to Gulbaz and tells him, "I didn't notice your compound when I first got here. It's huge. How big is it?"

"Well, ten acres, more or less, and you didn't have any shoes on. That tells me how much you remember!"

"It must have cost you a fortune to put a ten-foot wall around it."

"Yes, I spent all of my money and borrowed some to pay for the wall around my property. I did it for my children. They are not able to go outside, so I brought the outside here to them."

"You really are a good father."

Nick looks around and thinks this place is really magical. The pomegranate trees are in full bloom with orange-colored flowers. Apple, cherry, peach, and pear trees extend as far as the eye can see.

"What is that in the fields?" Nick asks.

"Oh, that's wheat. Traditionally, we plant wheat in the fall, and wheat is the first thing we harvest in early summer. That gives us a chance to plant two more times, things such as vegetables, which we dry for winter."

"What about poppies?"

"My father taught me to earn the honest way. I leave poppies to the Taliban to harvest. I believe in consistency. I have witnessed people leaving their traditional ways of living, which leads them to a shorter life. I tend to follow in my father's footsteps. I think that is the honorable way to live and to survive."

Nick is persistent in his questioning for many reasons. One, he finds Gulbaz to be different from others, especially considering what Afghanistan has gone through. Second, Nick wants to learn more about Gulbaz so he can work with him effectively.

"How do you harvest all this once it's time to pick the fruit and other things?"

"In Afghanistan, we have a volunteer system called *aasher*. Thirty-five to forty of us village men go to the orchards and pick the harvest every day until it's all done. Most of our fruit goes to Kandahar city, where we sell it to a processing company."

Even after all this time spent with Nick, Gulbaz has yet to pronounce his name correctly. Gulbaz gets frustrated trying to make sense of his name. One morning, he comes up to Nick and, head on, tells him, "Your name sounds strange. I am going to call you *Naikee*. It means *goodness*."

Nick does not mind Naikee as long as his new friend feels comfortable calling him that.

Naikee works side by side with Gulbaz every day, sometimes fourteen to sixteen hours, and he enjoys every minute of it. Gulbaz also enjoys working with Naikee and feels as if he has the son he never had. Conversation does not take place between the two. Mostly, they avoid getting too deep into political conversations, since Naikee realizes the limited scope of Gulbaz's world.

For Naikee, this time away from his family is the most difficult. He does not realize his despair during the day, but come the night and staying in the huge guestroom, loneliness chokes him up. He has no way of knowing how Lisa and the children are doing.

One thing that Gulbaz is always afraid of is that Molawee may one day force himself into the compound. Although Molawee is also a Pashtun, once any Pashtun is trained by Al-Qaida, the codes of honor automatically wear off. In desperation, Gulbaz brings a double-barreled shotgun passed on to him from his father and hands it to Naikee.

"What am I supposed to do with this?" Naikee asks.

"This is for your protection. I am afraid one day Molawee may try to force himself in and take you back. I want you to keep this close by."

"What are you going to do?" Naikee asks.

"I don't sleep too far from my Kalashnikov at night. You don't have to worry about backup. I am not too far. I am going to bring the Kuchi dog here by you, so if it barks, you know someone is trying to enter the house."

Naikee really appreciates Gulbaz's offer. He wants some company, and a pet will be a blessing in a lonely place such as this. Gulbaz walks back with an animal that does not look like a dog. The animal is held with two heavy-duty chains. The dog is pulling Gulbaz, a strong man, like a teenager who does not know how to handle a dog. Both the tail and ears have been cropped to the base.

Naikee has never seen such a mean, huge, ugly dog as this one. It makes bulldogs adorable by comparison. The Kuchi dog is in a defensive mode, with his upper lip retracted and almost all of his large teeth showing.

Do I really want to pet this dog? Naikee thinks. *It looks like a dog from a horror movie, enhanced digitally.*

With great difficulty, Gulbaz puts the ends of both chains onto a stick that is buried in the ground and secures the dog in place. "Try not to pet him. He will never get used to you and will bite you any chance he gets."

"I don't think I want to pet this thing you call a dog."

"I have had him for the past three years. This dog covers the entire compound at night, and so far in the past three years, he has killed three wolves," Gulbaz says proudly. "And one more thing—if you want to relieve yourself before sleep, do it before I release him because once he is free, the entire compound belongs to him." Gulbaz kept the dog chained all this time, and Naikee did not know about the dog. Now, Naikee needs to relive himself before the Kochi dog is released at night.

"Don't worry. I'll make sure to hold on for as long as possible. I sure don't want to be bitten by this beast."

By now, the nice, cool weather has turned to a dry, hot summer. Most nights, Naikee stays awake from the intense heat, despite the long work hours. Temperatures drop from 120 degrees in the afternoon to only ninety degrees by five in the morning. It is impossible to sleep inside during the summer nights. The guestroom has a stairway to the rooftop. After dinner, Naikee climbs to the roof to get a little breeze, even if it's a dry, warm breeze. One thing Naikee never witnessed in his years living in New York was the number of stars here in Uruzgan. There is no shortage of stars in New York, but the difference is that they cannot be seen because there are so many lights there.

Sleeping on the rooftop may offer some relief from the heat, but there is no way to escape the persistent swarms of mosquitos. With many water puddles inside the compound, there is never a shortage of mosquitos. Naikee covers his head and his entire body, but the mosquitos find a way to attack him all night long.

There is also a good chance of coming down with malaria from the mosquitos. Naikee is not exempt. At first, he thinks he may have come down with the flu. However, constant fever and weight loss are not flu symptoms. Gulbaz knows exactly what is wrong with Naikee. His guest sweats all night long, and his bed gets wet as if he has taken a shower in it. Naikee stays awake all night long to drink water and to prevent dehydration. Naikee may have spent many lonely nights since his captivity, but he has never felt more lonely, scared, and afraid of dying as he does now since he came down with malaria. Even with a minor flu, Lisa was at his side to pamper him and to nurse him back to health. Nick misses her more than ever.

I am not afraid of dying. But I am afraid of dying when I am thousands of miles away from my family. I want to see my wife and kids before I die, Naikee thinks while burning with fever.

The fever and the joint pain are incomparable to any pain Naikee has ever experienced. The best Gulbaz can provide is expired aspirin from the era of the Soviet invasion. Naikee's fevers and hallucinations worsen. Gulbaz fears the worst.

Life is lived in hope of the future. *I am not giving up on seeing my family,* Naikee tells himself. *I will get better, and I will see my family again.*

CHAPTER EIGHT

The Bravery

The next morning, Naikee forces himself to get up. He walks around and force-feeds himself with fresh fruits. Many days pass, and Naikee loses at least twenty pounds. Not only has he been away from work, but he also has been keeping Gulbaz from his work. The harvest is nearing, and Gulbaz cannot lose another minute because he may lose his livelihood without this year's harvest. Naikee slowly recovers from malaria and is able to help Gulbaz once again.

Harvest time comes, and Gulbaz hasn't invited anyone since Naikee entered his already complicated Afghan life. He wants to keep the village people away from Naikee, but the harvest is too big for only two men to handle. Besides, Naikee may one day leave, but Gulbaz has to deal with the village people for as long as he lives.

On an early June day, the village people knock on Gulbaz's door. Naikee has already cleaned the guestroom, but he is very nervous as Gulbaz asks him to open the gate for the men to come in.

Naikee knows that *nanawatai* is a very strong code, but he also knows that bad actors, such as Molawee Abdul Satar, also exist who have no regard for any Pashtun honor code. He trusts Gulbaz's reassuring looks and opens the gate.

The village people have been eager to see the infidel ever since his escape, but they didn't expect him to open the gate. The awkward stares make Naikee feel as if he is not wearing any clothing. He invites everyone in and tries to hug everyone in the traditional way.

Gulbaz directs most of the younger villagers to more physically demanding work because this prevents them from horseplay. He directs the mature boys to supervise and to cook for everyone. Gulbaz asks one of the elderly men to help him with the slaughter and cleaning of a sheep, as he has to feed all forty men. The harvest starts, and Naikee tries to keeps himself busy with things far from other activities, but the awkward stares drill through him, and he can't help noticing them.

Naikee by now speaks Pashtu fluently with a southern accent, and he surprises the villagers when he talks. Some younger kids approach him and ask him if he was born here in Uruzgan. He tells them, "I feel like I was born here," so he can keep the youngsters guessing and keep them in line.

The harvest ends with a grand meal, and the fruit gets loaded onto the trucks. Gulbaz and the other villagers can tell how much they will get paid for their harvest based on how many trucks are loaded. Gulbaz looks at the trucks as they are parked inside his compound and tells Naikee, "I had a good year. I still have the pomegranate to sell in the fall and the harvest of potatoes and vegetables."

After all the guests leave, Naikee goes to the guestroom and sits by himself while Gulbaz stands outside the gate and gets paid for his harvest. Naikee especially misses his wife and kids because of the youngsters he met today.

He sinks into deep thought. *Am I ever going to leave this place?* Now that he doesn't have any contact with Molawee, he has been completely disconnected from his family. He realizes that his family might think he's dead. *The tradeoff is good for me and bad for my family. I didn't know what Molawee's plans were. If I had stayed and let Molawee go through with his plan, I might not be alive today.*

The next morning, Gulbaz walks in early in the morning with breakfast.

Naikee asks Gulbaz if he is able to get a telephone. Gulbaz says, "What do you need a phone for?"

"I need to talk to my family."

"No, you can't get a phone."

"Why not?" Naikee asks.

"The Taliban have set up checkpoints on every road coming to this village, and if they find a phone on anyone, they will first break it and then beat the owner senseless. We used to have people here who worked for the government and the Americans, but not anymore. Don't take Molawee for a fool; he is a very smart and well-connected man. The bad things about phones are that they bring raids to our village and get many innocent people killed. Let us go outside and get some air because we both need it. I know you feel like a prisoner in this home, but I also have become a prisoner in my own home right along with you. Everything will work out, *inshallah.*"

Yes indeed, God willing that they will, Naikee tells himself.

In the days that follow, Gulbaz tries to stay close to home because he fears Molawee may be getting impatient, the way gossip circulates around the village, and will try everything in his power to break into his home and take Naikee. Gulbaz doesn't travel too far from his home, only to the nearby shop to buy essentials such as sugar, kerosene, tea, and salt.

The long summer days are joyful for Naikee. He likes to sit outside after he is done with his work. However, once nightfall nears, he gets depressed. *I don't know what it is about nightfall, and I don't know why I don't like it,* Naikee thinks. *I didn't feel like this at home. I still prefer the long summer days over short winter nights. The minute the night falls, I feel sad. Why?*

At home in the States, after dark, there was electricity. At home, he was able to watch TV, read a book, and use his computer. Here in Afghanistan, most of the people go to sleep right after nightfall because there is nothing to do.

Naikee enters the guesthouse and prepares to go to bed. Back home, he was able to fall sleep with no problem, usually within a couple of minutes. However, here, as a captive, thoughts of his family and his small children keep him tossing and turning all night long. The best he can hope for a good night's sleep is maybe five hours.

Tonight is not any different, and as usual, Naikee is unable to sleep. He looks at his digital watch, the only prized possession he still holds since the beginning of his ordeal. It is 12:25 a.m. He can hear the Kuchi dog squealing restlessly but not barking. Naikee gets up to have a look outside the window. The full moon allows him to see very well. The Kuchi dog is running around the front gate and sniffing.

What's with him? Naikee thinks. *Why is he so restless tonight?*

Naikee doesn't think of much of it and goes back to bed.

Naikee leaves all the windows open, and he can hear the crickets chirping. He can hear dogs barking in the distance, and that makes Gulbaz's dog act strangely. Naikee once more gets up to see what is making the dog so restless tonight.

The dog then starts to bark, and Naikee becomes alert. He pulls out the double-barreled shotgun and loads the chambers. He slowly walks to the door, which has direct access to outside the compound, and checks if it is locked. Sure enough, the door is locked, but he can sense someone standing right outside because the dog is agitated, running from side to side.

Naikee notices Gulbaz in the distance, pointing to him to stay down. The door is pushed a couple of times, and Naikee knows without a doubt that someone is there. Naikee puts his finger on the trigger, lying down at a forty-five-degree angle from the door, as he knows very well not to stand directly behind the door.

Gulbaz calls the dog, who runs toward his master. The dog stops barking and sits by Gulbaz. Naikee is scared but keeps his cool. He knows very well not to lose his composure. Panic can kill a man fast.

The first shot rings out from the left side of the main gate. Gulbaz starts shooting at the man on top of the wall with his Russian-made AK-47.

Gulbaz moves from his position, running toward the guesthouse. Without a doubt, it is Molawee's men, and they are after Naikee.

Soon, multiple shots blast through the small door, and two men enter the guesthouse. Without hesitation, Naikee shoots the man in front. The second man turns back and takes off right away.

Gulbaz enters the guesthouse and asks Naikee, "Are you okay? You are not shot, are you?"

"No, I'm okay. I'm not shot. How about you?"

"No, I am good. Finally what I was expecting, it just happened," Gulbaz says. "I am pretty sure they will never try to come back again as we sent a very strong message tonight."

Gulbaz turns the kerosene light on to see and assess the damage. The man who was shot is still bleeding but is dead. He and Naikee pull the dead man from the guesthouse and lay him on a spare, old wooden bed.

Gulbaz closes the dead man's eyes and wraps his scarf around his chin and head to close his mouth. Gulbaz then starts reading a short prayer and asks Naikee to check the other man he shot who was sitting on the wall.

The force of the bullets flying from Gulbaz's AK-47 had forced the other man to fall outside the compound, and the blood running down the side of the wall confirms he is either dead or severely wounded. Either way, he does not pose a threat, as he would be unable to climb the ten-foot wall again.

Neither man is able to go to sleep in the wake of a very tense night. Both Naikee and Gulbaz sit by the gate with their rifles loaded in case there is another firefight. Instead, the night turns into day without further incident.

Gulbaz goes outside the gate to see if anyone has claimed the dead man. The man is gone, leaving a puddle of blood staining the dry, sandy soil. Gulbaz looks around and does not see anyone. He walks back in.

It is around ten in the morning when someone knocks on the door. Gulbaz right away opens the door to see who it is. It is the mullah from his local mosque.

"I am here to claim the dead body of a man in your house."

"Do you know who he is?" Gulbaz asks.

"He is not a local man. He is from the Kandahar area. His family was notified this morning, and they are here to claim him."

Naikee is surprised at how simply this matter is resolved. He thinks, *Instances like this in any other country of the world require some kind of government involvement. However, here in Afghanistan, Kabul is the only province where the government has some authority on a very limited basis. Everywhere else, matters are decided by local tribal councils, the warlords, the Taliban, or the local mullahs.*

Most of the village people understand the situation well. They know who did it and why they did it, and if you are still alive and have a dead man in your house, you just have to give it to the right person, and the case is pretty much closed.

"I brought two of the local boys with me to help with the body," the mullah says.

"Very well. There is the body." And with that, the case is over. No one is going to ask Gulbaz what happened or how it happened.

Naikee, totally surprised, shakes his head and goes inside the guesthouse to clean up. He first needs to fix the broken door.

For Molawee Satar, this is another devastating blow. One thing Molawee is sure of—he will never be able to pull off something stupid like this again because, despite his power in the area, tribal elders will hold him accountable for his actions if he repeats the same mistake.

In light of this incident, Haji Abdul Qader desperately calls a *jerga* (grand council, a local meeting to resolve local matters) to put a lid on the situation and come up with a solution so that such an incident will not take place again. He sends his son to many of the tribal elders' homes and finally to Gulbaz's house as well.

The next day, as Gulbaz takes an afternoon nap, he hears a loud knock on his door that wakes him up. He immediately gets up, puts his hat on, and runs toward the door. Millions of thoughts go through his mind as he walks toward the door. He opens the door, and it's Haji Mohamed Qader's son. Gulbaz greets him and asks him to come in.

Qader's son comes in and says, "I can't stay long. My father has called a *jerga* at your home, and he asked me to inform you. He said the *jerga* will be held after the Friday prayers."

"What is it about?"

Qader's son says, "I think it's about the infidel."

Gulbaz tells him not to call him *the infidel*. "His name is Naikee."

"Okay, it's about Naikee."

"Okay, tell your father I accept the *jerga*, and all members are welcome to my home."

A sudden *jerga* such as this one makes Gulbaz very nervous. He thinks Molawee may be pressuring his community to turn Naikee back over to him. He is between a rock and a hard place. Gulbaz is an honorable man and under no condition breaks Pashtun codes.

Naikee is kept away from it all, but his sixth sense detects trouble. He knows Qader's son has come and that *jergas* are not held on such short notice unless they are important.

On Friday afternoon, Gulbaz walks to the local mosque, and after the prayer, some twenty men come back to his home. After a meal, Haji Mohamed Qader once again starts with a speech of goodwill and reminds everyone that this *jerga* has been called about Naikee and the well-being of the community.

Naikee eagerly awaits the results. He knows why the *jerga* was called: because of the incident that occurred the other night. He can detect the discomfort on Gulbaz's face because he will be affected by the decision made too, equally if not more.

Haji continues his conversation and finally mentions that this *jerga* was called because they are being pressured by Molawee Abdul Satar. He has vowed to revolt against all the tribes. "We are powerless against Molawee's ruthless army. We have enough problems as it is. The last thing we need is a revolt from Molawee and his men."

Gulbaz asks, "So what is the solution? I will never turn Naikee in. That is against our tradition and against everything we stand for. I am an old man, but I will singlehandedly defend Naikee with my last drop of blood."

Haji Qader says, "Don't get me wrong; I and everyone in this room will stand in support of you with every man we have, but we are all looking for a peaceful solution."

Gulbaz is a simple man. He has never had to face a challenge this great. He sweats profusely and has no idea what to say.

An elder from Bazan Kelai, Zardad Mama, usually sits quietly and listens but never says anything. When he speaks, he surprises everyone. Whenever he wants to say something, he never actually asks to speak. The *jerga* members simply notice his body language and know Zardad Mama is about to drop a bomb. His solutions are quick, to the point, and very effective.

Haji Qader, along with other *jerga* members, notices Zardad Mama's body movement and asks him, "Zardad Mama, do you want to add something?"

The elder clears his throat, runs his fingers through his long, white beard, and looks at Gulbaz. "I have never hated anyone as much as I hate Molawee Abdul Satar. There was a time when youngsters listened and elders made decisions, but now elders are silenced and youngsters force everyone to whatever their hearts desire. What has this society come to? This is not the way our forefathers hoped for us to become. We don't accept Pashtunwali, and we don't follow our religious teachings. What have we become?"

All *jerga* members nod their heads in agreement and wait for what Zardad Mama really wants to say.

"The reality is," Zardad Mama continues, "we can support you in your nobility, and we all think you are a great man. I think if Naikee had knocked on anyone else's door on that day, no one would have turned him down, and we all would be facing the same reality as you are facing today. But one thing is clear—we all have to deal with Molawee Satar the same way you are today. He is an evil man, and what I am about to ask you may surprise you. I am sure this is the only solution, and it will get Molawee off of our backs peacefully."

Gulbaz and the others are eager to hear what Zardad Mama is really thinking. The elder again composes himself, and complete silence pervades the large guestroom.

"Gulbaz, you have to accept Naikee as your son-in-law! He has been converted, and our religion teaches us that we do not discriminate against anyone's color, race, or nationality."

Mumbling starts around the room. Gulbaz's jaw drops in total disbelief. Haji Qader intervenes and brings the *jerga* to order, saying, "It is really controversial, but I couldn't have come up with a better solution myself."

Gulbaz leans back and feels as if his soul has just left his body. He can't believe what has just happened. What *jerga* concludes is what everyone must comply with. There is no way out of this decision for Gulbaz. He must accept the *jerga* members' wishes.

Haji Qader announces the end of the day's *jerga* and tells Gulbaz, "We will allow you until next Friday to absorb all this, and we will call a new *jerga* next week to finalize it. Do you accept?"

"Yes," Gulbaz says. "I accept."

Haji Qader makes one more announcement to the *jerga* members. "What has been said here should be kept confidential. Once Naikee becomes family to Gulbaz, Molawee cannot do anything about it."

The guests start to move toward the exit. Gulbaz barely finds the strength to stand up. He then leaves the room and says good-bye to each guest as they leave.

Naikee has been waiting outside the entire three hours while the *shura* took place, but Gulbaz doesn't even see him standing in front of him now.

Gulbaz walks on to the main house and lies down. Naikee starts cleaning the guestroom and thinks, *Whatever just happened here is not good. I have never seen Gulbaz this sad.*

The next morning, Gulbaz wakes up and brings Naikee breakfast. He sits down in total silence and is not able to look at Naikee. Not a word comes out of Gulbaz's mouth. This makes Naikee even more nervous because he doesn't know if he is being turned back to Molawee or what. He politely asks Gulbaz if he is okay.

Gulbaz tells him, "I am not feeling well. I am going to rest today. You can work by yourself today. You know what to do." Gulbaz leaves the room.

Gulbaz walks to his room and for the first time shuts the door behind him. He has never shut the door since Shaista and Toor were born. Toor, his five-year-old blind son, is sitting in the middle of the room and calls, "Baba! Baba!"

Gulbaz needs some kind of comfort from someone and calls his son to sleep next to him. He holds Toor tight and tells him, "I wish your mother were alive. I can't make all the decisions by myself."

Gulbaz thinks, *Naikee has a heart of gold. He was the one who taught me how to plant things a new way, which has made the harvest almost twice as big, and has used water efficiently. He has been working with me side by side like a son and always has a smile on his face.* Gulbaz knows he likes Naikee, and he can be the son he always wanted.

Gulbaz wakes up in the afternoon. Shaista, his daughter, has prepared lunch as usual. She slowly and softly calls, "Baba, lunch is ready."

Gulbaz reluctantly gets up, picks up the lunch tray, and starts walking to the guestroom. He and Naikee eat in silence. Naikee pours a cup of green tea for both Gulbaz and himself. Gulbaz takes a sip and puts his cup down.

He tells Naikee, "You may have been wondering what the meeting was about yesterday."

Eagerly, Naikee says, "Yes, very much."

"I have been through a pretty tough life. Thirty-five years of war. Buried my father and mother. Two of my brothers and I have dealt with and lived every minute of it all. I have made many tough decisions in my life. But none of that compares to what I have been asked to do this past Friday. I told you I have two children."

"Yes, you did," Naikee replies.

"Their names are Toor and Shaista." Most Afghans use one name.

Naikee becomes a bit alert as Gulbaz mentions his daughter's name. Afghans never mention their female family members' names. Naikee doesn't remember seeing Shaista even for a brief moment. She obviously milks the cow and does all the work around the house—cooks, washes, prepares food for large groups of guests, makes bread—yet it seems as if all these things get done automatically without Naikee catching a glimpse of her. How does she do it?

Gulbaz continues his conversation. "In order for me to keep Molawee off my back and stop him from harassing the entire community, you have to become part of my family."

Oh no, you are not, Gulbaz. You are not asking me what I think you are, Naikee thinks.

"I have turned down many requests to marry my daughter over the past three years because I know boys nowadays are careless and irresponsible. This is the most difficult moment in my life, to ask a man to marry my daughter. I think this is the only way we both live, and this is the only way I can live with some dignity."

"But I am already married," Naikee says.

"This would be your second marriage, yes? You are permitted to marry up to four women at the same time, so what is the problem?"

"You live here in Afghanistan. You don't have to worry about that. The only thing you have to worry about is if you can feed them all."

"I think neither one of us has a choice. It is marriage, or one of these days, Molawee will break into my house and kill all of us. The next *jerga* is taking place next Friday. We don't have much time to think about this. You as a man, do I have your word?"

Naikee is speechless. He asks Gulbaz to allow him a moment. "How old is your daughter?"

"I think she is sixteen."

Oh my God. A polygamist and an underage bride. Wow, Nick, you've really done it this time. You're going against everything you believe in.

Gulbaz, as a simple man, does not have the faintest idea how the world really works. He is a man of narrow vision and does his best to justify matters according to his limited knowledge. Gulbaz goes on to say, "God willing, once things get better here, you would be able to go back and forth to see both of your wives, and it will be your duty to take care of all of your wives."

Naikee thinks, *Things have been bad for the past thirty-five years here in Afghanistan. I don't think things will get better anytime soon in this country.*

Naikee looks at Gulbaz, a proud man asking him to marry his daughter, but he also looks like a broken man. *We all have that moment in our lives when we get so beat up, we have to play our last card. Indeed, Gulbaz is perhaps at that junction in his life right now.* He has no choice, and Naikee is also in the same boat.

"What's next?" Naikee asks.

Is this constant surprise going to end anytime soon? Naikee thinks. *A man can tell himself enough is enough and give himself up to circumstances, but do I have the right to put others in danger? I was the one who knocked on his door, changed his life forever, and he took me in. I was selfish saving myself, and now I have changed this man's life forever. What is right and what is wrong? I have no idea anymore. Is it survival? But at what cost?*

Naikee tells Gulbaz, "I will answer your honor with my honor. You have my word."

Gulbaz walks out of the room and enters the main house where, by tradition and religious duty, he must ask his daughter if she agrees to a marriage. The father and daughter never have any real conversations, only if a guest comes and Gulbaz tells her to cook. Shaista tells him if she needs any household items, and he buys them from the nearby shop. But she senses the discomfort in her father's eyes. They never talk about their real feelings, wants, and needs.

Gulbaz asks Shaista to come because he has something very important to tell her. She comes in and sits by the door. He starts by saying, "All girls must one day leave their father's home and make their own home. I think you are the right age to get married."

Shaista doesn't say a word and understands the process. The process is to say yes, and there are no ifs, ands, or buts about it. The choice one's father makes is the life one gets stuck with.

"But it is my duty to ask you if you agree to this marriage," says Gulbaz.

Shaista has no idea who the person is, and, as is tradition, she has never met him and does not know his name, how old he is, or what he does. She looks down and doesn't say anything. But Gulbaz knows that traditionally, silence always confirms agreement.

Gulbaz tells her, "Your marriage will take place in two weeks."

At all times since Shaista was born, Gulbaz has kept a false hope that he may be able to keep her in his home forever, just as any father around the world would want to do. If she were a son, he definitely would have stayed home with him for as long as he lived. Most girls here in very rural Afghanistan get married at age fourteen or younger. Gulbaz has kept Shaista for as long as possible. At this point, if he keeps her any longer, the people of the village will start talking, and that is not something Gulbaz is looking forward to. Now he is going to be left with a blind son, and Gulbaz may have to think of getting married himself. Who is going to take care of Toor when Shaista leaves?

Shaista gets up and carries on as if nothing has happened. Gulbaz tells himself, *I hope I have made the right choice. How things change from peace in my home one day to what I am about to face and what is coming next. Life is often unpredictable and full of surprises.*

Naikee is ashamed, disgusted, and angry. Nothing he tells himself can convince him to feel otherwise or justify his actions. At this juncture in his life, his direct and indirect actions have their own minds. He no longer decides his own destiny. His destiny is predetermined, his decisions are made for him, and his situation has created unfavorable conditions and life-changing experiences for others.

CHAPTER NINE

The Honor

Despite the fact that Naikee gave his word of honor to Gulbaz, guilt overwhelms him to the point where he feels paralyzed. Naikee is not able to eat, sleep, or rest. All he had hoped for was that he would one day be freed and be able to go home to his family with some dignity intact, but circumstances had different plans for him.

It has been over a year now since Naikee was kidnapped. Did he give in to circumstances by his weakness, or was it all pure survival instinct? He is not sure. All he says to himself is, *What if I had done it differently? Would I be in the same mess? If I explained it to Lisa, would she understand? No. No matter how good my intentions were and how bad my circumstances are, my wife will never understand. She will always feel betrayed by and disappointed in me.*

The following Friday, Haji Qader and the *jerga* members gather in Gulbaz's home. The ceremony starts with a prayer, followed by a direct question to Gulbaz. "What have you decided?" Haji Qader asks.

Gulbaz takes his hat off, places it on his knee, and scratches his head uncontrollably because he still is not sure and is unwilling to give his daughter up so easily. Sweat rolls down his cheeks and drips down his short, white beard as his close relatives, cousins, and distant cousins await his decision.

Gulbaz reluctantly opens his mouth and says, "This has been the most difficult decision I have ever made in my life. As you all know, I have been a widower for more than five years, and my only daughter is my life. Now I have to give her away. All daughters one day have to go to their own homes, but one thing I take comfort in is that at least I will still be seeing my daughter here in my home every day. My answer is, whatever is best for our community is best for me."

Haji Qader turns to the other *jerga* members and says, "Gulbaz has made a wise choice, and I think this will help us get Molawee Satar off our backs."

The *jerga* concludes that the wedding will take place next Friday. Haji Qader says, "We should again keep this meeting confidential until the wedding is over." Everyone in the meeting agrees with Haji Qader's decision and is relieved to hear Gulbaz's decision.

Haji Qader is a wealthy man. He takes full responsibility for the wedding expenses and adds, "I am going to represent the groom since he does not have any family here."

As the day of the wedding approaches, the burden of guilt almost cripples Naikee. He is a man of principle, he does everything by the book, and he is an extremely ethical person. Now he allows himself to go with the flow, whatever it takes to survive, yet he is still a man of principle. He is no different from his soon-to-be father-in-law number two, Gulbaz. His life was also changed dramatically in the past few months, and neither one of them has had a choice but to surrender to circumstances.

The fateful day arrives, and the women from Haji Qader's family and other tribes flock to Gulbaz's house. They wear colorful dresses. The women come early to prepare Shaista for her wedding. This is the first day ever that she doesn't have to do anything, just sit down and look pretty all day long.

Most of the men are preparing a meal for everyone. Haji Qader brings four sheep, some fifty chickens, and lots of rice for the feast. He also brings new clothes for the groom. Haji Qader brings a pair of *shalwar kamise,* new sandals, a new hat, and an Afghan-style turban. Haji Qader has also invited the village barber to give Naikee a haircut and beard trim.

Naikee walks to a small bathroom adjacent to the guestroom where the boys have left him a large bucket of water, a new bar of soap, and his new clothes neatly placed nearby.

Naikee wishes for the ground to split open so he can disappear or for a natural disaster to occur so he can get away from this most awkward situation. However, reality cannot be avoided by wishful thinking. He is going to face it like a man and let the flow take him wherever it does.

Naikee slowly puts on his clothes and walks out to the guestroom. His heart is beating fast. He feels completely out of place and out of his usual character. The only person sitting in the guestroom is Haji Qader. He greets Haji Qader and sits down.

Haji Qader looks at Naikee with an awkward smile and tells him, "I kept the other guests out of the guestroom so you don't feel uncomfortable. I am going to tie the turban on your head because I assume you don't know how." Naikee agrees.

After placing the turban on Naikee's head, Haji looks at him and says, "If I didn't know you were an American in advance, I wouldn't have thought you were in a million years unless I was told otherwise. You look exactly like one of us."

Naikee picks up a small, round mirror and looks at himself. "I really do look like someone who was born in Uruzgan."

Molawee Satar's men immediately report to their leader that a wedding is taking place at Gulbaz's. He doesn't have the faintest idea what is really happening. However, he is really upset because he wasn't invited. He knows Gulbaz has a grown daughter, and she is probably getting married, but to whom? No one ever bypasses him because no one in this village is allowed to do anything without his approval. This situation creates a new dilemma for Molawee.

The actual marriage, or *nekah*, takes place before the food is served. The guestroom fills with men only. Most men have picked hand fans from the wall to cool off with. Most whisper to each other, as they are witnessing something this odd for the first time.

One of the *jerga* members, Mullah Bari, calls Naikee to come closer and sit in front of him as he writes the marriage certificate on a small lap table. Mullah Bari calls two witnesses in the room, as required for *nekah* to take place. Two men volunteer and come forward. Mullah Bari asks them to state their names for the record.

"I am Mohamed Tooriali."

"And I am Abdul Wasai."

"The groom, can you state your name?" Mullah Bari asks.

"Naikee."

"And your father's name?"

Naikee gets nervous because his father's name may sound very strange, but he realizes his father's name, Ibrahim, is also common among Afghans. *Oh, what a lucky break*, he thinks. "Ibrahim."

"You, Naikee, father's name Ibrahim, take Shaista, Gulbaz's daughter, for your wife?"

Millions of thoughts go through his mind, but one thing he is sure of—"no" is not the answer.

"Yes, I do."

Mullah Bari asks the witnesses to put their thumbprints on the marriage certificate. Naikee also puts his thumbprint on the certificate.

The witnesses and Mullah Bari walk toward the main house to ask Shaista the same question. The bride is traditionally not allowed to see the mullah or the witnesses. Shaista and some of the women are sitting behind a curtain.

The mullah asks Shaista, "You, Shaista, the daughter of Gulbaz, take Naikee, son of Ibrahim, to be your husband?"

She for the first time realizes whom she is marrying. As an Afghan girl, she has said yes to her father, not in so many words, but it was a yes. She, like millions of other Afghan girls, has no power to choose or think for herself. Just like other decisions, this one was also made for her, and she answers, "Yes, I do."

Mullah Bari shoves the certificate under the curtain and asks her to put her thumbprint on the last available space. Mullah Bari and the witnesses walk back to the guestroom and congratulate Naikee on his marriage. Naikee goes around the room and hugs everyone as required by tradition, and Haji Qader asks the men to start serving the food as Friday prayer closes in.

Naikee can't wait for the party to end because he feels as if he is going to pass out. He sits there in the most awkward moment of his life with a fake smile on his face.

Naikee remembers his wedding back home to Lisa, with music, lots of booze, and dancing. *Can this wedding get any more awkward? Here in Afghanistan, music has been banned since the mullahs took over in the 1980s. There is no difference between a funeral and a wedding*, Naikee thinks.

Naikee maintains a fake smile and does his best to make everyone feel welcome. All the guests leave one by one. The room empties, and so does the house. Everyone leaves by 1:00 p.m. Naikee starts cleaning up the guestroom. As of today, he is not required to sleep in the guestroom; he is family now. A separate room has been prepared for him in the main house. He was wishing for everyone to leave, but going into the main house is a challenge of its own. He takes his sweet time to clean up. However, cleaning the guestroom will end at some point, and Naikee will be on his way to see and live with his new bride.

By sundown, the last women have left the main house. Haji Qader's wife, who was keeping the bride company, also leaves when her son is ready to take her home. Soon Naikee has to face reality and go home. Yes, his home. Now he actually has a home and a wife waiting for him.

Naikee slowly walks toward the house, but his heart beats very quickly. He stops a few steps short of the door and thinks, *I should wait some more. Maybe it would be a good idea for me to go back to the guestroom and see if it still needs some more cleaning. Perhaps the plantation needs me. I will volunteer to pick harvest at someone else's home despite the dangers. I am even prepared to turn myself in to Molawee Satar if I can avoid the awkwardness of this situation.*

None of these childish thoughts will help Naikee ditch his new life. His choices are limited within this ten-acre compound.

He thinks he is betraying Lisa with every step closer to the house. He is Nicholas Blake, an American, legally married to Lisa, with two beautiful children. What is he doing here anyway?

Gulbaz walks out of the house and says, "Why are you hiding like a thief? Come in. This is your home now."

My home? My wife? This is really more difficult than I thought it would be, Naikee thinks.

Naikee walks in, and Gulbaz tells him, "See? That room on the left is your room, and the one on the right is mine."

Naikee nods his head in agreement and slowly walks toward the room. He wants to knock on the door, but he tells himself that would be very strange. He takes off his new sandals and then walks into the room.

Shaista is sitting in one corner, awaiting her husband's arrival. Her face is covered. Her husband is to take the veil off of her face. The room is lightly decorated with golden strings. On one side of the room, a newly sewed mattress and comforters are neatly laid. Nick can see Shaista's hands decorated with henna, and her feet are hidden under her dress. The room smells good, and everything around the room is neatly arranged. Shaista is wearing lots of bangles on both her wrists and makes a sound every time she moves her hands.

Naikee sits as far away from Shaista as he can manage. He doesn't know how to break the ice or what to say to his new bride. She acknowledges her husband's presence mostly by light body movement.

Two hours pass, but Naikee is still in the same spot. Shaista takes her veil off and waits some more, but Naikee doesn't have the guts to even look at her. He grabs a pillow and lies down with his head turned to the wall, sleeping as far away from her as he can manage.

Shaista starts crying, turns the kerosene light off, and goes to bed alone. Naikee realizes she has waited for this night all of her life. She doesn't understand what is going on in her husband's mind. As a matter of fact, she doesn't know anything about her husband except that he is supposedly Molawee's American captive. Naikee thinks, *I am from a different culture, the kind of culture she will never comprehend for as long as she lives. We are two people from two different worlds. We have absolutely nothing in common.* Naikee burns with guilt and confusion and thinks, *What have I done? For a woman on her wedding night, this couldn't be more insulting and humiliating.*

No reason will justify her rights as a wife and as a woman. Marriage is for life for most Afghan girls. *It is like she does not have the right to be happy even for a brief moment,* Naikee thinks.

CHAPTER TEN

The Guilt

D ays go by. Shaista gets on with her daily household chores, and Naikee gets busy helping Gulbaz in his fields. They never sleep together. He sleeps in his corner, and she sleeps in her corner. It becomes the norm, and they learn to live under the same roof but never acknowledge each other.

Fall arrives, signaling the end of planting and harvesting. Soon Naikee and Gulbaz both have the entire winter to do nothing, just eat, sleep, and plow the plantation for next year before the snowfall.

Molawee Satar feels powerless and very unhappy because the decision for Naikee and Shaista to marry was made behind his back. He hopes someday Naikee will feel comfortable enough and come out of the house, and he will take him back and deliver him to his buyers with Al-Qaida. However, Naikee is too smart and knows well that his first mistake will be his last one. *Besides, I'm on ten acres of land. I have more than enough space to move around and don't want more adventure since my first one landed me in the situation that I'm in now.*

Winter arrives. The days grow shorter, and both Gulbaz and Naikee spend more and more time at home. The entire family eats together, but Naikee likes to drink his tea in his room. Gulbaz brings Naikee a hand-wound rechargeable radio that was distributed by the Americans for free so people can listen to news and Afghan music. He gives it to Naikee so he can listen to news and music that are broadcast from a nearby military base. This becomes the highlight of Naikee's day, and he enjoys it.

One night, Naikee, as usual, eats dinner with Gulbaz, Shaista, and Toor, Gulbaz's blind son, and then he gets up and walks to his room just as he does every other night. Shaista brings him his tea. She always sits close by and drinks her tea, too. Despite their lack of communication and acknowledgment of each other, they somehow expect each other's presence and awkwardly enjoy the indirect relationship. Naikee turns on his radio and listens to the eight o'clock news, and Shaista sits quietly. Naikee for the first time asks Shaista, "Have you ever gone outside the gate?"

But Naikee mixes up his feminine and masculine pronouns as he speaks Pashtu. She giggles and corrects him. He also notices his mistake and starts to laugh.

Shaista tells him, "No, I have never been outside the gate."

He unintentionally turns his head in total surprise and asks, "Why?"

After being married for four months, Naikee sees his wife's face for the first time, and for a moment, he is speechless. She also notices him seeing her for the first time. He can't believe how pretty she is. She doesn't have any makeup on, but she looks like a beauty from a storybook. Now it's an awkward moment for her; she is being stared at by a man who hasn't been there since their marriage. It almost feels unnatural to her to be stared at by a man.

She gets up and is about to leave the room, but Naikee says to her, "Don't leave. Please, sit down. I ... I ... want to talk more ..."

Shaista is quite embarrassed and reluctantly sits down. She unintentionally acts as if this is her first time meeting her husband. Naikee looks at her. Shaista looks down shyly, but Naikee keeps looking at her face. She has beautiful, big, green eyes. From the little hair showing under her head scarf, he can tell it's very dark, and her hands look as if she has never worked a single day in her life. Naikee thinks, *Her name, which literally means beautiful, sure fits her.*

It is love at first sight. She, too, feels something she has never felt before. She, too, for the first time feels the person behind the shadow of this so-called husband. She does not mind the attention she is getting right now after four long months of an artificial marriage, but she does not know how to present herself.

Suddenly, Naikee is able to see and hear every positive quality about her. She is shy, never speaks unless spoken to, and is very soft spoken. He is attracted to the sound of her many bangles on both her wrists.

Days go by. At first, Shaista is reluctant to talk and doesn't know how to present herself, but Naikee constantly talks to her and asks her questions.

"What do you like?"

"What is your favorite color?"

"What kind of music do you like?"

But for Shaista, all these questions seem silly. She doesn't understand because all she knows is what she has seen within her father's ten acres and the house she was born in and grew up in. Besides, questions like these embarrass her. Shaista has never had friends to talk to. Nor has she seen things on TV to relate to what Naikee is saying. Nevertheless, she enjoys the attention.

Shaista slowly opens up and tells Naikee about her life and how she misses her mother. "My mother was the center of my and my father's life, but now she is gone. I admire the sacrifice my father made for me and Toor."

Naikee soon realizes his wife's world is very small and untouched. Things that he is trying to say will not make sense to her. He needs a new approach, a new way of winning her heart. She seems to be the kind of person who does not need diamonds and gold to be won over. All she needs is a good husband, a man of honor, and a good provider.

I need to speak to her in a way she will understand. I don't want to make a fool of myself, nor do I want to confuse her, because what I am trying to say to her is from my past life. I have to learn how to place myself in her small world. Naikee keeps telling himself, *I am responsible for this woman now. I don't know how I am going to be judged once I get out of here, but she deserves the best from me.*

As the long winter nights go by, Naikee and Shaista become inseparable. They talk late into the night and sometimes early morning. The light of love can be seen in their eyes. Naikee teaches Shaista how to read and write and also teaches her English words. She is eager to learn English because she wants her husband to be impressed by her.

Shaista keeps bringing up babies in her daily conversations, and Naikee keeps telling her, "When the time is right." She doesn't understand what that really means.

Naikee thinks he one day will get out of here and take her with him. *But how?* he asks himself. *Take her where? Marriage aside, how would I explain babies?*

Winter turns into spring, and once again, the huge compound turns into a beautiful, dreamlike garden. All the fruit trees are in full bloom with colorful flowers. This plantation doesn't need planted flowers; it seems to have been touched by God's hand because its beauty is beyond human imagination. Naikee enjoyed city life in New York and many other parts of the United States. However, he could not have imagined that isolation could also be beautiful in the right place at the right time—and with the right person in a beautiful garden like this.

Naikee is now completely cut off from the rest of the world. His family back home is under the assumption that he must be dead. Naikee was once a loving husband and a loving father. Now he doesn't think much about his family back home because he has come to accept this life as his real one. Sometimes when he is too happy with his current life, he wants to share it with Lisa, but that is out of the question. He doesn't know how to explain any of this, and he knows none of it will make any sense to Lisa.

Naikee once again gets busy helping Gulbaz in his fields. He picks wildflowers that grow along the streams inside the compound and makes sure he takes a bunch every evening when he returns home. Naikee thinks, *My marriage to Shaista turned into a love story that is written about only in novels. But this love is new, pure, and untouched by external forces. Meaning in life can be found anywhere, even in a war-torn country such as Afghanistan. Finding happiness depends on a person's perceptions and open-mindedness.*

Naikee thinks to himself, *I can't believe a man, a complete stranger in the middle of nowhere, can be loved and be this happy. It's almost magical.*

Naikee wants to tell Shaista more about the outside world, how he wants to take her places and wants her to see the world, but he doesn't want to make promises he cannot keep. Reality always haunts him, and he knows too well that once he gets out, he will not be able to take her with him. But he is madly in love, so in love that he overlooks his other marriage with Lisa. At times, he doesn't even remember he is actually married to another woman.

Naikee always notices helicopters flying overhead at high altitude. But he has also noticed a noisy, small plane flying overhead the past few days. He asks Gulbaz, "Is it usual for this plane to be flying around this area?"

Gulbaz replies, "This plane has an eye on it, and they can see us. Usually when this plane flies for a few days, a raid is imminent within the next day or two. I call it 'the buzzing one.'"

Naikee doesn't think much of it and carries on with his work. He always thought Afghans were unaware of technology, but they do know how capable the foreign forces are from their own narrow perspective.

Naikee is especially keen to go home and spend more time with Shaista. He does his chores and picks flowers as he always does. He can't wait to go home. Shaista also misses Naikee and makes all kinds of excuses to go out and see him. The couple talk late into the night and go to sleep as the kerosene light runs out of fuel.

For Naikee, Shaista is the most uncomplicated woman among those he has dated throughout his life. Her wants and needs are so simple, and he doesn't have to try very hard to please her or to understand her.

As the first light of daybreak shines through the single window, a loud knock on the front gate wakes Naikee up. His first instinct tells him, *Finally, Molawee has decided to break into the house with his full force this time.*

He runs out to the hallway, and Gulbaz is also awake. Gulbaz tells Naikee, "Stay in, and do not go outside. I am going to see what is going on."

Naikee asks, "Is it Molawee?"

Gulbaz says, "No, it's a raid on our house. I will go out and try talking to them."

Shaista is terrified and holds Toor in her arms. She holds Naikee's hand tightly and tells him, "Stay inside. Please don't leave me by myself. I am really scared. I do not want to be seen by other men."

Naikee stays behind, and Gulbaz walks quickly toward the gate. The loud knocking continues. An interpreter's voice echoes in the crisp early morning air. "Open up! It's a raid! We want to ask you a few questions!"

Gulbaz opens the gate, and an army of men with full gear enters the large compound as helicopters hover above and make very low passes.

Through an interpreter, an officer orders Gulbaz to ask the entire household to come outside and sit down as his men conduct a search of the house. This is the most undignified moment for any Afghan to face. Naikee gets the full picture of how humiliating this process is. He can really feel it now that he is married to a conservative Afghan woman. However, he also realizes that resistance can get people killed.

Gulbaz runs to the house and asks everyone to follow the orders. Shaista sits as close as possible to Naikee and trembles uncontrollably while holding Toor in her arms. She covers her face with her head leaned on Naikee's shoulder.

The officer slowly approaches Naikee. He appears to be holding a picture in his hand. He comes even closer and takes a good look at Naikee. The strange man terrifies Shaista, and Toor can feel the presence of the strange man although he is completely blind. Through an interpreter, he then asks Naikee, "Who are you? What is your name?"

Naikee hears English for the first time in months and knows very well why they are here. The officer, with an Australian accent, asks him, "Are you Nicholas Blake, mate?"

Nick replies, "Yes, I am."

"I wouldn't in a million years have been able to tell from your picture that it was you, if you hadn't spoken. You sure have changed. What is your wife's name? I have to positively identify you."

Nick gets his wives mixed up for a moment, but he knows what the officer means. "Lisa," he replies.

"And your children?"

"Ashley and Fargo."

"What did you do for work?"

"I worked for the UN in New York."

"Well, it's your lucky day, mate. You're going home, Nicholas Blake. We are here to rescue you. I have to take him, too." The officer points to Gulbaz.

"You don't have to take him," Nick says. "He's the reason I'm still alive."

"I'm sorry, but it's our procedure to do so."

"But I have to take her with me." Nick points to Shaista.

"No, we don't want to start an international incident here. We're not allowed to take women and children."

Nick is furious, but he is not able to say that she is his wife.

The officer is confused as to why Nick would want to take an Afghan woman with him. "Is she sick? If she's sick, I can let my medic take a look at her."

"No, she's not sick," Naikee replies.

"Okay, then I want you to follow that man. He'll lead you and the other man to the helicopter. We don't have much time. We need to get out of here before the insurgents start shooting at us."

Shaista starts screaming when she sees Naikee leaving. She hangs onto her husband, the love of her life, the only person she has ever loved. "Please don't leave! I am going to die without you!" she screams in Pashtu.

The Australian officer looks surprised but has no clue what is going on. Naikee asks the officer for a moment to talk to Shaista.

He walks to the house with Shaista holding onto his hand. Naikee tells her, "I am coming back for you." He tells her in English, "I love you." These are the only English words Shaista knows, and she knows what they really mean. "Trust me. I am coming back for you, even if it's the last thing I do in my life."

But no words of assurance can convince Shaista. She knows that this is the last time she will ever see her husband.

"Please stay inside," Nick tells Shaista. "You must be strong for all of us. You need to be strong for Toor. He needs you. I need you, and your father needs you."

Shaista lets Nick's hand go and drops to the floor, screaming. Nick walks out.

Nick and Gulbaz both are escorted to the helicopter, with Gulbaz's hands tied behind his back and a black mask pulled over his head. The convoy of five helicopters takes off one after the other and flies over Gulbaz's large compound. Nick looks out the window. Shaista runs as she looks up. There is nothing Nick can do to comfort her. He has just lost the person he loves the most—so innocent, so beautiful, and so caring. The Australian officer hands Nick a pair of earplugs to protect his hearing from the Chinook's deafening noise. Gulbaz rides without earplugs.

The helicopters land at Tarin Kowt base, capital of Urzgan, after a half-hour flight. Bob, Nick's boss, is standing outside to greet him. They take Gulbaz away, and Nick assures him that he will be released and sent home as soon as possible. Gulbaz doesn't say anything and walks on.

Bob tells Nick, "I have arranged for you to speak to your wife and kids. You can take as long as you want. I'll wait for you outside. They've been waiting for you for a long time, pal, and it's nighttime there."

Nick thanks Bob and walks into a typical plywood army barrack with the video call already set up. He closes the door behind him and takes a moment to absorb what has just happened. He doesn't know whether to be happy to see his family or sad for losing one. Things are happening so fast that he is not able to absorb everything. Two hours ago, he did not in his wildest imagination expect to see his other family.

Nick breaks into tears when he sees Lisa and his kids. He sobs uncontrollably, and Lisa and his children are also overwhelmed seeing Nick after a long time.

"I'm sorry, baby, for letting you down," Nick says. "I didn't mean to do it, but it just happened."

"You haven't done anything wrong, honey," Lisa says. "It's all right, sweetie. You're alive, I'm in good health, and the kids are doing well."

For Nick, this is awkward and confusing, and he feels guilty both for the life he has with Lisa and the life that just ended two hours ago. How is he going to find peace, and how is he going to resolve this unplanned life?

"Honey, I need to go because I'm flying out this afternoon. I'll see you all in a couple of days, hopefully."

"Okay, take care of yourself, and we have a lot of catching up to do." Lisa ends the call.

Indeed, I have a lot to catch up on and a lot of explaining to do as well. This is only the beginning, Nick thinks.

After the short and awkward video call, Nick goes outside and asks for the officer who rescued him this morning. He is Officer Henry Gibbs, Australian Army Special Forces. He is debriefing his soldiers, and when he sees Nick, he starts walking toward him.

"Well, hello, Nick. Did you have a chat with your family?"

"Yes, but I have to talk to you about the man you brought with me."

"Oh yes, what about him? We're required to hold him for seventy-two hours, mate."

"Well, if not for him, I would have been dead a long time ago. He took me into his home and accepted my asylum, *nanawatai.* He has a disabled five-year-old boy and a daughter at home. He needs to go home now."

"Well, I don't want to promise you anything, but I'll talk to the people who are processing him."

"Thanks," Nick says.

After ten minutes, Officer Gibbs comes back and tells Nick, "Although it's against our regulations to release someone this soon, you claim to know him, and we're going to make an exception and release him now."

Nick thanks him again and asks if he can see Gulbaz.

Officer Gibbs tells Nick, "Yes, you can see him."

Nick runs to the holding cell and sees Gulbaz sitting there, sad and uncertain about what is going to happen to him. Nick approaches him and tells him, "*Ta korta zai.* You are going home. I want to assure you, I am coming back, and I will take all of you with me."

But Gulbaz knows too well that will never happen.

As standard procedure, the processing staff hands Gulbaz his belongings and fifty dollars for his unplanned travel as a goodwill gesture. But Gulbaz, a proud man, throws the fifty-dollar bill at the man and is escorted out of the compound.

Nick walks outside, where Bob is waiting for him.

"Hi, Nick. I've been looking all over for you. Where were you?"

"I had some business to take care of."

"Why don't you go and take a shower? And please shave. You look like a local. I have a flight arranged for you in a couple of hours. It will take you to Kandahar, where your flight to Dubai is at 1500."

Nick finds the bathroom and quickly showers since his flight is soon. He holds a razor and shaving cream in his hand. He looks at his beard. He can still feel Shaista touching it. *Having a beard is not a crime. I'm keeping it,* he decides.

Nick doesn't feel the full effect of his separation from his beloved wife the entire journey up to the point when he lands in Dubai. But the reality sets in when he takes the long flight to New York. He cannot believe that a flight home, what he always craved, would be so burdensome. As the large triple-seven Boeing roars down the runway and takes off, he realizes that his year-and-a-half journey of being kidnapped, his grand escape, and his marriage to the most beautiful woman have just ended.

Nick has never thought the reverse of what he used to think until now—that leaving his home in New York is possible and that leaving Afghanistan is even more difficult. How his presence in Afghanistan has changed so many lives, changes he cannot undo. That he is unable to see Shaista again is unbearable. One thing is for sure—the long flight home will give Nick plenty to think about. He is in a state of shock right now. The reality may kick in once he is home—his real home. Or is it?

CHAPTER ELEVEN

The Separation

The long flight from Dubai to New York gives Nick plenty of time to think, but there are more questions than answers. Meeting his family is the least of his problems, but it surely is a challenge of its own. He knows he will have to deal with the awkwardness and new beginning with Lisa. But at the same time, he needs to tell the truth, the painful and strange truth. Lying is not Nick's style; he is known for his honesty and integrity.

But honesty aside, how am I even going to explain my actions? How am I going to justify what happened in the course of my ordeal in the past year and a half? Will I be able to patch up things with Lisa, or will I be perceived as a selfish, unfaithful person who broke all of his own rules for the sake of survival? Nick wonders.

I can only hope for things to turn for the better, as I know the reality will be much different once I get home. I didn't plan this. It just happened, Nick thinks, consoling himself.

Indeed, reality will be different at home. No matter how hard he tries, he cannot put Shaista out of his mind. He wants to jump out of the aircraft and somehow magically land back in her arms. Nick knows very well that his imagination will get him in trouble once he gets home.

Why am I subjected to such torture? I didn't ask for this life. But what fault do Lisa and my kids have in this ordeal of mine?

Nick's mind keeps racing and wanders in directions he never imagined possible.

I don't know what Shaista is thinking and feeling right now. This is her first time away from me. What can she be thinking right now? Am I a selfish pig to be thinking about my forbidden marriage when I am on my way home to see my real wife and children?

Nick is torn between his life in America and his simple, exciting, scary, and lovely life in Afghanistan. Nick is in trouble once more. He is going to have a hard time adjusting to his old (or altogether new) life again.

His fears become more real as the aircraft makes its initial descent. His mixed feelings over being free and again facing a real life, the life he left behind, and what he has been through the past year and a half send through him a kind of fear he has never faced.

I need to be on my best behavior and at least pretend that I'm in a normal state of mind. This is my first encounter with my family after more than a year and a half. They have been through the same ordeal as I have. They don't deserve to be slapped with the truth right away. I'll try to prepare Lisa slowly but surely, and I hope the kids will someday forgive me. After all, I was the one who made the wrong choice to leave on an adventurous ride with Charlie.

Nick prepares to face his family for the first time, his real family.

The fifteen-hour flight finally comes to an end, and Nick makes his way to the baggage claim area. He is picking up the same bags with the same clothes that Lisa packed and folded a year and a half ago. He wishes he were like his clothes, untouched by external forces.

Nick walks out to the passenger welcoming area. He easily picks out his family. They are waiting for him with a lot of flowers, and most of his friends and even some of his neighbors also have shown up to welcome him. They are waving American flags. He is a hero to most. He has survived. The way Americans use the word *hero* makes one think that heroes are only born, nurtured, and living in the United States. However, Nick was the victim of unfortunate circumstances beyond his control. He does not think he is a hero.

Lisa and the kids run past the security lines and hug him as the local and national media cameras snap pictures and videos, recording his every move. Reporters are screaming questions. Nick certainly expected his family to greet him, but he completely forgot that he would have to face the media, and he is unprepared.

Nick faces the cameras with his family at his side. He hears questions coming from reporters relating to his time in Afghanistan. He doesn't know which one to answer first. He raises his hand, and everyone awaits a dramatic response from him.

A momentary silence surrounds the airport-echoing lounge, followed by his comment. "As you all know, this is my first encounter with my family after long months of waiting. So all I am going to say is that I am glad to be back, and no matter how bad things get, one should never give up on life. I am no hero. Anyone in my position would have done the same things I did to survive, and the rest is history."

After saying the politically correct thing, Nick starts walking out of the lounge and doesn't answer another question. The reporters scream for a more dramatic response from him so they can play it over and over on the six o'clock news for days.

Nick's kids are glued to him. He is sure enjoying this special moment. Both Ashley and Fargo have grown up.

The short ride from the airport ensues with a few typical questions directed to his children. "How is school? Have you made new friends? Did you two drive Mom crazy all this time?" The answers are also typical, either yes or no.

When he enters his New York apartment, Nick feels as if he never left home in the first place and none of the events of the past year and a half ever occurred.

In the days ahead, Nick makes every effort to spend more time with Ashley and Fargo. Lisa keeps her distance and allows him space to recuperate from what he has been through. She does not ask him millions of questions, as she herself is a very sensitive person. She has also been advised by kidnapping victims not to pressure Nick into revealing too much or to expect him to return to his old self in a matter of days. Rather, he should be allowed to find himself, and with therapy, he will recover slowly but surely.

The only thing that bothers Lisa is his long beard. She asks him to get rid of it. But he keeps telling her, "I will when the time is right." Lisa has no idea what that means and when the right time is.

Nick spends most of his nights out in the living room, staring at the walls and thinking. He will never return to being free after his marriage to

Shaista and living on ten acres of land. Now, the best getaway for him to free his thoughts is to go to the living room of a two-bedroom apartment. But his train of thought travels only one way. The only thing on his mind is Shaista. The worst part of it is he doesn't have any contact with her. He often thinks, *What happened to her after I left? What did she go through when I left?*

At this point, the US troops have pulled out of the most important regions of Afghanistan, leaving a power vacuum to be filled by the Taliban. Southern Afghanistan has fallen into the hands of the Taliban, and the same is true of the eastern part of the country. Pakistani troops are largely in charge of the Pashtun regions of Afghanistan and most likely are integrating the entire Pashtun region into the northwest frontier.

One thing that really interests Nick after his arrival at home is the CNN news. He watches the news with an intense interest. His take at this point as a diplomat is that the nightmare most Afghans have been afraid of has finally come to reality. The country will be divided for the second time after one hundred years or so. The Northern Alliance will control the northern part that connects to the central Asian countries, and the southern and eastern parts will be controlled by Pakistan. Western Afghanistan is taken over by Iran. However, the same style of infighting that uprooted the country's infrastructure in the 1990s has once again returned. The US Army is still holding major bases, such as Kandahar, Shindand, Khost, and Jalalabad. However, the United States is in talks with the Taliban to turn over these bases to the Taliban peacefully.

The monster that was created by the United States is finally unleashed in full force, Nick thinks. Street fights between different factions of the Afghan government are ten times worse than they were in the 1990s. As far as the rest of the country is concerned, warlords are dueling it out village by village, town by town, and city by city. People loyal to one warlord are being hanged by the others to make a brutal statement.

The corrupt, uneducated, disloyal society will finally get what is coming to them—the division of their beloved country, Afghanistan, into a northern and northwestern Pakistani frontier. What a shame! Afghans surely have failed to take advantage of the coalition forces' occupation. Instead, some have become loyal to Iranian mullahs, and most Pashtuns are slaves to Pakistan's ISI. Nick angrily mumbles.

Lisa sees Nick's condition getting worse, and nothing she says makes him happy. She takes matters into her own hands and seeks professional help. She brings it up in conversation every chance she gets and convinces Nick to seek help for the sake of the children and their marriage. He knows what his problem is, but he agrees to see a doctor.

Nick opens up almost immediately and talks freely to his psychiatrist, Dr. Brown. He tells her everything from the time when he first landed in Kandahar to the last minute of his ordeal, but with some parts missing in between—actually a big part missing in between. His marriage to Shaista.

As weeks pass, Nick makes regular visits to Dr. Brown's office. But the doctor makes it clear she doesn't see much improvement in his condition. Nick almost immediately breaks down and cries every visit. At first, Nick's psychiatrist sees this pattern as normal since he was away for so long. However, she notices that there are parts of the story of his captivity that are missing, and she tells him so.

The next session, Dr. Brown, without an opening statement, asks Nick directly, "What are you hiding, Nick? I see more pain than you have admitted to. Usually at this stage of treatment, I see some improvement, but you're hiding something. What is it? You can tell me."

Nick excuses himself and walks out of Dr. Brown's office. *Yes, I am hiding something,* he thinks. *Something that no one can help me with, something that no one will ever understand.*

Nick stays awake late into the night and sleeps all day long. He forgets to pick up his children as Lisa tries to keep the family together. He does not have the courage to go to work or be at all functional.

Soon Nick realizes that this can't go on forever. The pain is far greater than anyone can imagine.

Nick wishes for Shaista to come and for all of them to somehow live together.

Why can't a man love more than one woman? Is it against the law of nature? I don't think it is. Why can't the law have an understanding or at least make an exception in my case? I can't leave Shaista to die out there without me. What kind of man in his right mind would leave a person whom he loves dearly and never think about her? Should I just close my eyes and pretend that it never happened? I want justice. I want justice for myself, for Lisa, for my children, and for Shaista. I want justice.

Well, justice from whom? The government? Society? The world? God? Who is Nick seeking justice from? A reasonable person would naturally convince himself he is a victim of unfortunate circumstances. But Nick is madly in love. In his vocabulary, *rational* does not exist.

As a confused man in love, rationality and reasoning escape Nick. He mostly thinks and justifies things with his emotions, not his brain.

I need to go back, and I need to get Shaista out of there. I may be seen as the worst parent and husband, but I promised her I would come back for her. I can't leave her there. She will die without me, and I, too, will die without her. I must rescue her just as I was rescued. I may be judged by many, but I can't escape my own judgment.

In reality, right judgment escapes Nick, and he gives in to his emotions. The real reason he has lost judgment is that he can't live without Shaista.

Once I get her out of there, I will somehow explain all this. I will hope for the best, and I will let nature take its course.

In the coming days, Nick struggles to find a justification for his cause. Nick is restless. His wife of nine years and his kids still depend on him despite his abnormal state of mind. For them, he is their husband and daddy, and that's all.

Nick tries his best to write something wonderful in his defense and somehow convince his children he needs to do this. But in reality, he must be a man and once and for all tell Lisa and the kids the truth. But no matter how hard he tries, he is gutless in facing reality. He decides to go back to Afghanistan for now and deal with Lisa and the kids once he gets his other life figured out.

Nick sits at his desk, pulls out a paper and pen, and writes Lisa a note. Tapping the pen against the paper uncontrollably, Nick doesn't know how to begin or how to put it nicely. He finally decides to write a short explanation of what really happened.

Nothing I can say will satisfy Lisa, he thinks. *I'm a coward, and I'm destroying what I built over so many years. Lisa aside, my children have no fault in this. They will judge me for as long as they live.*

In his note, Nick explains everything that happened. He does his best to justify his actions, but the fact of the matter is no one will judge him more than the woman he has been married to for years and had children with.

CHAPTER TWELVE

Emotional Journey

Despite the chaotic state of Afghanistan, Nick sets off on his dangerous mission to save the love of his life. He packs very lightly this time; the only thing he takes with him is his *shalwar kames*. He looks around the house with his children's pictures covering the walls, and without thinking about who is going to pick them up from school today, he heads out the door.

Nick takes the first flight to Dubai. The next flight to Afghanistan does not exist since no one recognizes Afghanistan politically. Moreover, the chaotic state of the country prevents many airliners from flying in and out of Afghanistan.

This situation creates a brand-new dilemma for Nick. He is stuck here in Dubai. He either needs to fly to Pakistan and on to Afghanistan at his own risk, or find a way to go to Iran, Uzbekistan, and Tajikistan. However, every country has its own risks. Pakistan is out of the question; since he is an American, he will be killed right at the airport. Going to a central Asian country will leave him too far from southern Afghanistan.

Nick's best bet is to find a way to sneak into Iran as an Afghan. Then he can travel eastward into Herat and on to Uruzgan. But how will he mange to find a smuggler?

Nick is unfamiliar with Dubai, even though he has been through the city many times and has spent many nights here. *I need to go to Daira Bazaar. I'm sure I'll find many Afghans there.*

Nick heads out to Daira Bazaar, which is located in downtown Dubai. It's a short walk from his hotel room. He walks past packed storefronts in search of an Afghan.

The Afghan drug trade is not a new phenomenon. Dealers smuggle drugs through Iran and on to Turkey, Eastern Europe, and the United Arab Emirates for its close proximity to South Asia. For Nick, it shouldn't be difficult to find an Afghan drug dealer in Daira Bazaar. After all, it is known for its African and Afghan drug dealers.

The smell of pot late at night attracts Nick. He follows it. He sees a bunch of grown, mixed-race men sitting in the back alley smoking pot from Shisha. With Dubai being a police state, these men are taking a big chance smoking in public. However, Nick's long beard is a passport to the underworld of downtown Dubai. His appearance is common among Kandahari men. He is not feared, and the friendly men invite him over for a smoke.

He greets the men. *"Aslamualikum."*

"Walikum aslam habibi." The men greet Nick in one voice and make room for him to sit. The smoking men aren't sure where Nick is from and start speaking to him in Arabic. Nick puts a few words together but presents a disclaimer for his weak Arabic language abilities.

One man asks Nick in Arabic, as Nick resembles a Kandahari, "Tell me, what language do you speak? Arabic, Urdu, Pashtu, Dari, or Farsi? We have someone from everywhere here, and we can get a conversation going."

Nick greets the man in Pashtu. The man gets up and hugs Nick. "Are you from Kandahar?"

"Yes," Nick replies.

"Oh, my countryman, where did you come from? Here, why don't you start smoking? I am going to bring you green tea." The man walks away from Nick.

For Nick, this is a lucky break. He has found an Afghan sooner than he expected. The man pours a cup of a green tea from a thermos and asks Nick, "Have you eaten? I can get you food from a restaurant or from my home, which is not very far from here."

"No, I have eaten, but I really appreciate your offer."

This is a typical Afghan gesture of hospitality for his countryman to make, and Nick is joyful at a breakthrough, at least for now.

Nick spends hours speaking to the men. Most are shopkeepers or laborers from many different nations enjoying a hot, muggy evening together. The man Nick just met is Abdul Baqi, who has owned a shop here in Dubai for thirty years. He still has some family in Kandahar, Afghanistan, but most of his children and brothers are busy working right here in Dubai.

Nick opens up a conversation by saying, "I need to see my family."

"Oh, you don't live here in Dubai?" Baqi asks.

"No. I was here working for many years, but now I have to go to Kandahar. I have my family in Uruzgan, but I don't know how to go back since there are no flights to Afghanistan."

Nick has to lie. This is a good opportunity for him to make some connections with these men and in particular with Abdul Baqi, who has been living in Dubai for many years.

"Why not work here some more, and, *inshallah*, things will get better in Afghanistan soon?" Baqi asks Nick.

"Well, I need to go back because I have family who need men at home since things are really bad there again."

"I see what you mean. Why don't you spend a night here with me? I will see what I can do in the morning."

"I don't want to burden you at this time. I will come back in the morning and see you," Nick replies politely.

"Okay, very well. Come back tomorrow morning. I will call some people and send you home as soon as possible."

Nick thanks everyone and heads toward his hotel room. He realizes the false hope all Afghans hold in their hearts, the hope of the past thirty-five years that has never materialized into reality, that one day Afghanistan will return to its normal state.

Nick walks back to his cheap motel room since he needs to be careful with his money. He has yet to find a way to raise some cash. However, in his situation, making money and finding a job are not on his mind. He wants to get out of this expensive city as soon as possible or he might run out of money before reaching his final destination.

Upon reaching his motel room, Nick feels an urge to call home, to talk to Lisa to see what happened after his unannounced departure. His cowardly act bothers him a great deal. After all, he may never get the chance to talk to or see his family in the United States again.

I didn't have the guts to face Lisa and the kids when I was at home, he thinks. *If I call them now, it may give them a little hope or at least let them know I'm alive.*

Nick picks up the phone, dials the number, and hangs up. He's not sure what kind of reaction he will receive. He lies on the bed, staring at the ceiling for many hours and thinking. *I need closure. If I don't call her, that will be an even more selfish and cowardly act. I need some peace before leaving. I need to know how my family is doing.*

Nick finally picks up the phone and dials the number again. The phone starts ringing. His hand trembles as the familiar US ringtone enters his ears. On the third ring, he wants to hang up but holds onto the handset as sweat starts to trickle down his long beard. On the fourth ring, Lisa pick up and screams, "Nick! Nick! Is that you? Please say something, Nick!"

Nick doesn't know what to say and sobs silently as Lisa screams continuously on the other end. Nick can hear his kids calling for him as well, and he can feel Lisa instructing them to say it.

"Dad, we know it wasn't your fault. We know what happened to you. Please come home. We need you. We miss you, Dad. Please ..."

"I'm sorry, baby. I didn't want to leave like that. I love you, and I love you, kids, so much," Nick says.

"We can work it out, baby. Please don't go to Afghanistan, because things are so bad there. You can go back once things are better."

"Please, let me do this. I have a responsibility that my life created for me unintentionally. I have to take care of that, and I will be back. I promise." Nick sobs. His tears, sweat, and nose drip down his long beard. He hangs up the phone.

Well, that wasn't closure, but at least Lisa and his children know he is still alive. For Nick, nothing he can say or do will take away the guilt he feels about everything that has happened in the past two years. His life has been an emotional journey.

Nick puts his head down on the pillow, closes his eyes, and thinks some more—the kinds of thoughts that mostly are far from reality, the kinds of thoughts a ten-year-old boy would conjure in his wildest imagination, where he is in full control of a nonexistent world.

Nick falls asleep sometime in the early hours of the morning. He wakes up around nine o'clock. He quickly gets up, as he is supposed to meet Abdul Baqi about his trip to Afghanistan.

This is it, Nick thinks. *I think this Baqi guy is going to set me up, and I'll be on my way as soon as today. I'd better check out of the hotel so I can save some money.* He packs up his belongings in a small black duffel bag.

Nick walks quickly. It must be 125 degrees here in Dubai. Nick finally arrives at Baqi's shop. Baqi is speaking to some men and waves to Nick, saying he will talk to him in a minute.

Baqi starts walking toward Nick with a smile on his face. "*Salam*, brother. Nice seeing you again."

"You too, Brother Baqi. How are you?"

"Good. I was able to talk to some old friends. They, *inshallah*, will take you home. I want you to hang out around here because my friend will come later today. I don't know what time."

"Okay, I will. I am going to buy some things for home. Do I have time to do that?" Nick asks Baqi.

"Yes, of course you can. I am sure someone at home will be expecting something," Baqi replies jokingly, referring to a woman at home.

Nick walks away smiling. He needs to lock up his IDs and other papers so his real identity is not discovered. He walks to a nearby bus station and locks up his passport and other identification. He then tucks the receipt under his vest pocket to keep it well hidden in hopes of retrieving his identification once he makes it back to Dubai with Shaista.

Nick walks back quickly, as he is afraid he may miss this opportunity. Baqi tells him to join him for lunch.

"You never told me your name."

"Oh, my name is Naikee." Nick uses the name given to him by his Afghan father-in-law.

"Okay, Naikee, you are one lucky man. If you had met me one day later, you would have missed the trip."

"I am very grateful to you, Abdul Baqi. I don't know what I would have done without you," Nick replies.

"As my countryman, you need to do something for me. You need to carry some of my friend's things with you, packing it in your belongings."

Nick becomes alert. *What is it he wants me to carry back?* Nick thinks to himself. *Drugs don't go back. Oh, it's the drug money he wants me to take back!*

"You don't have to be concerned. We do this all the time. I consider you as my friend, and I trust you with my friend's belongings."

Nick does not have any choice but to accept taking the drug money back to Afghanistan. With his hand going toward his mouth, eating with his new friend Baqi, he remembers the American cliché, "There is no such thing as a free lunch."

Nick accepts Baqi's offer, and Baqi asks Nick to stay at his shop for the night because his friend will pick him up early in the morning. "I will leave the air-conditioning on for you tonight because it gets really hot at night. I will see you in the morning."

Nick spends most of the night awake, thinking that he is one step closer to Shaista. However, in the process, he has become a drug dealer, too, among all the other names people and some of his close friends call him. The only person who can really understand what he is going through is himself. No one has gone through what he has in the past two years. One thing is for sure, he is the most honorable man. Not many men measure up to him. He gives the name of man true meaning. No one is perfect. In the course of his honorable deeds, he may have broken many hearts and hurt many. But honor aside, he is actually and truly in love. Whether his honor or love is stronger, one can only judge from his or her own point of view.

In the early hours of the morning, Nick hears a loud knock on the store's large, rolling gate. He opens the back door. Baqi and some men are talking outside the store. Nick greets them, and Baqi asks Nick to stay inside.

After a couple of minutes, two men walk in with Baqi with a large, rolling suitcase. Carrying a suitcase is a good alternative to a briefcase and duffel bags, as they would stand out. The men pull out a sweatshirt and matching pants. The clothes are like a Hollywood costume to make an actor look fat. The double-layered costume is filled with cash for Nick to wear. It will make him look like a fat man, but it is a perfect fit, so it will not make anyone suspicious that it is a cash-filled costume. Nick does not have much choice but to wear the costume since this is his one and only chance to get to Afghanistan. Wearing such a heavy costume in 125-degree heat will be highly uncomfortable, and it might get even hotter when he travels through the dry desert in Iran and Afghanistan.

"Why don't you put this on and tell me how you feel?" Baqi asks Nick.

Nick puts the costume on and wears his normal clothes on top of it. It is a perfect fit but must weigh around 120 pounds. "It's heavy!"

"Well, you are a strong man. You can handle it," Baqi tells Nick, smiling. "Now that you have your new body on, I am going to instruct you on what is going to happen. One, do not act suspicious. Two, don't get separated from your group. Three, make sure you have enough water at all times."

Baqi's friend adds, "Anyone who attempts to escape or intentionally attracts law enforcement will get shot in the head. Do you hear what I am saying?"

"Yes, loud and clear, and I completely understand," Nick replies.

"Now, let's go," says Baqi.

The drug runners are the best at their job. They know how to find desperate men in their most desperate times and use them. For Nick, this is as desperate as it can get. This is his only chance, and he cannot mess it up.

"If you think the Dubai police are tough, wait till you meet the Iranian border patrol," says the drug kingpin. "They are corrupt, they hate Afghans, and they are ruthless. My advice to you is don't make any eye contact with them if we run into them. Do not smile, do not speak Farsi, and do not try to speak to them in any way, shape, or form. Just shut up, sit tight, and I will handle it. In most cases, they are glad Afghans are leaving their soil; however, they are also aware of this operation. You are going to travel with four more men. Try to stay close to each other, and always keep an eye on each other. Do you understand?"

"Yes, I do," Nick replies.

Nick sits in the back of the box truck. For the first time, he feels how difficult it is for poor Mexicans when they cross the border to the United States, what kind of danger they go through to make it to the land of opportunity and prosperity.

After a short drive, the box truck makes another stop and picks up four more very nervous and anxious men. Nick doesn't even get the chance to greet them because the back gate closes so fast. The day turns to night with the slam of the back gate. The only thing Nick notices about the men is that they also look very fat, just like him, with thin faces.

The truck makes many stops. Nick can tell the driver is stopping at signal lights. Dubai is not a big city. The forty-five-minute drive finally comes to a stop, and the back gate opens up.

"Hurry up. Walk fast but don't run. See the freight ship? Walk there and get on board without talking to anyone. I have arranged for you five to get on board. They are about to load the ship. The crew is going to leave a six-by-six wooden crate for you all behind the many large crates. Make the best of it and try not to make a lot of noise. You are going to eat, sleep, and relieve yourselves in the same place," the driver of the box truck says quietly.

This reminds Nick of his captivity in Afghanistan. The only difference is that he was held against his will then, and now he is willingly putting himself in the same situation for the sake of love and honor.

CHAPTER THIRTEEN

The Underworld

The freight ship is located in Sharjah, not in Dubai. The distance between Sharjah and the first Iranian (Bandar-e Abbas) coastline is about eleven hours by ship. Nick and his new friends will have to keep quiet for that whole time and try not to have any bathroom emergencies for the duration of the slow ride. After arriving in Iran, the freight ship must be unloaded first before Nick and his fellow smugglers can get off the ship without being detected.

Nick remembers his first crush on Lisa. Every once in a while, a smell or a time and place brings those memories back to him. As he sits in a six-by-six freight container, the smell of the beach gives him that same sensation. He remembers the good times with Lisa. His current actions are taking him farther from her, but Nick still likes the smell because it gives him hope that one day, when he gets back and gets thing sorted out, he will be able to make up with Lisa, and things will be the same as they were before his unfortunate ordeal of the past two years. At the same time, this sensation he feels right now makes him want Shaista that much more.

The ship finally starts moving after being still for six or seven hours. It is really difficult for six men to move around in this space. Whatever happens from this point on, they have to bear it and take it like men. None of the men know each other. They have been coached not to talk to each other or anyone else. They all are very frightened and tired, and the hot, muggy air doesn't make it any easier or more comfortable with their 120-pound suits.

The gentle rocking of the ship back and forth makes all the men very sleepy. Nick has been awake for many hours since his arrival in Dubai. He witnesses each man go to sleep, one by one.

I don't know who they are or what their backgrounds are, but no matter how violent they are or what kind of criminal mind they have, they sure all look innocent when they're asleep, Nick thinks.

Nick leans back onto his duffel bag. He closes his eyes and falls asleep. The ship makes its slow journey to Bandar-e Abbas.

Nick wakes up, feeling intensely thirsty. He picks up his water container and takes a conservative sip so he won't run out of water before being able to get more. The warm water makes him even thirstier, but he puts the container down despite his overwhelming thirst.

A gentle bump of the ship confirms their arrival at the port of Bandar-e Abbas. Nick's box mates also feel the bump and wake up. It will be many hours before Nick is able to get off the ship.

It must be around two in the morning when the freight is moved from the ship. This is the most critical moment for Nick and his box mates to keep very quiet. They are not going to walk off the ship. The box will be moved onto a truck. Somewhere along the way, Nick and the other men will be able to walk out of the box.

The freight box is loaded onto a truck. The box once more is on the move, but there is no word from Abdul, Baqi's friend. All the men patiently and quietly sit in the same positions as before. As an Afghan, getting caught by Iranian authorities will automatically mean being hanged or shot on the spot without a judge or jury.

The truck makes a brief stop. Nick can hear the voice of Baqi's friend speaking to someone. The truck moves again and this time stops for good. The engine shuts off. The box gets moved with the help of a crane. The crane unloads several more containers and finally moves away from the truck.

"Are you all still alive?" asks a familiar voice.

Nick and the other men reply, "Yes, we are."

"I will have you moved in a minute. Be patient."

"Okay," all the men reply.

Several minutes pass. The man returns with a crowbar and opens the box. The men walk away one by one, wobbling and trying not to trip. The man who freed them does not want to waste time and asks everyone to be ready for the next leg of their journey in a couple of hours. "We are going to eat, and if you need to relieve yourselves, now would be a good time."

The next leg of the over-1,700-kilometer journey is by pickup trucks, which will take Nick and the rest of the men through Iran's deserts into Pakistan and finally to Kandahar, Afghanistan. The trucks used are called *Aaho*, which are American-made Dodge Ram pickups from the 1960s.

At four in the afternoon, the lead man whom Nick met in Dubai returns. He is serious-looking with absolutely no smile. He never introduces himself and obviously has no intention of doing so. Some of the men who are accompanying Nick call him in Pashtu "*de apemo mesher*," which means "the leader of opium." The name sure fits his facial description—lean and mean, with no emotional expression for one to read. He is all about business.

The men are separated onto three different vehicles and sent at three different times. The drug runners do not want their precious cargo to get caught all at once. If one of them is captured, the other two may still have a chance to make it to their final destination.

Nick is in the last truck with the kingpin. The pickup truck is filled with lots of diesel. Nick can tell the truck has been modified with large tanks. In the middle of the truck bed, a large water tank has been secured for long journeys such as this one. One thing that surprises Nick is that he finds a large number of MREs (Meals Ready to Eat) under the bench-like seat in the back of the pickup truck. The years of American occupation of Afghanistan and the years of the Pakistani government hijacking trucks on their way to Afghanistan have provided these precooked meals among many other items intended for the US Army that are found, bought, and sold all the way to Iran and other Afghan-neighboring countries.

Normally, the distance between Bandar-e Abbas and Kandahar is 1,700 kilometers. However, drug smugglers don't travel the normal routes for fear of being detected by the Iranian border patrol.

The rough ride begins for Nick. The kingpin and a driver sit in front. The ride takes them on unconventional paths that are known only to drug smugglers and their special drivers with a keen sense of direction. The drivers have traveled these routes many times. Usually they start at a very young age, riding with their father or relatives. The pay is very good, but the risks are great. The life expectancy of a driver is not more than two years tops.

Nick sits back and tries to make the best of it. The scorching heat with his costume on makes it impossible not to sweat. Bandar-e-Abbas is known for relative humidity as high as 65 percent during hot summer days. Nick grabs his container and fills it with water. Pouring some on his head and face provides him some temporary coolness. The pickup truck's top is covered with a tarp. The intense heat of this part of the world has really taken a toll on the tarp, creating many peepholes all over the beat-up tarp, but it does allow some air to circulate through the truck bed.

A couple of hours later, the sun is about to set. Nick can see the sunset through the cracks and many holes. Nightfall will bring some relief from the heat.

The driver does not stop during the night. The drive continues into the early morning hours, and the truck makes a short stop at the Pakistani border. The intense desert heat is noticeable even at four thirty in the morning. The sunrise will surely make matters even worse. The rough ride has made Nick's every bone hurt. He is glad the truck has made a stop after ten hours of pulling an all-nighter.

The kingpin walks to the back of truck.

"We are going to spend the entire day here," the kingpin tells Nick. "Try to get some rest because we will pull another all-nighter as soon as the sun sets. Eat something and drink lots of water."

Nick is tired, sweaty, and hungry. He grabs an MRE and heats it using the kit available with all packages. It is magnesium dust mixed with slat. When water is added to the mixture, the oxidation of magnesium accelerates, creating heat. He had an MRE before in his days in the army and a couple times in Iraq and Afghanistan. It tastes absolutely marvelous, eating a hot meal in the middle of nowhere. He finds shade under a bushy area, and the driver lays a camouflaged cover over the truck to hide it from the Iranian border patrol.

The intense, scorching desert sun heats up the area instantaneously. There is not much Nick can do to escape the heat. However, he is so tired from the rough ten-hour ride, he falls asleep right away.

For Nick and his company, the dangerous part of the journey is almost over. Once they enter Pakistani territory, the driver will pay his way out. Pakistani authorities are known for being the most corrupt in the world. However, crossing to Pakistani territory from Iran is still extremely dangerous.

Nick wakes up a few minutes past four in the afternoon. The driver is awake and greets Nick. He has made green tea and invites Nick to join him. The tea session passes without a word exchanged between the three men. No one wants to reveal himself.

"Eat something," the kingpin tells Nick. "We are going to leave in a few minutes."

Once more, the truck starts moving with Nick in the back by himself. After a half-hour drive, the truck makes a sudden stop. Nick becomes alert. The driver walks to the back of the truck and asks him, "Can you get the shovel from the back of the truck? We have to bury the dead."

Nick has no idea what the driver is implying. "What dead?" he asks.

"You will see," the driver replies.

The stench of rotting bodies is unbearable. There must be five young Afghan men shot by the Iranian border patrol, probably the previous night. The driver knows it was the Iranian border patrol because the bodies' mouths have been filled with sand, and all of their belongings have been taken.

"Their fathers and probably widowed mothers send them to Iran so they can earn some money. They come here to die the most gruesome death at the hands of the Iranian government. They also call themselves Muslims. Death to coward Iranian pigs!" the driver protests angrily.

The scene is a sobering reminder of how worthless human life can be. The driver is especially bothered by this because he sees this act repeated every time he passes by.

Digging in the sand is not that hard. All the dead are buried, and total silence falls onto the already very silent group. For those who are still standing, life goes on as usual.

The driver says a special prayer, and they all move on. Nick is bothered by this gruesome act and thinks, *The relatives and parents of the young dead men will never know the full story of their loved ones and how they were killed. They will probably wait for their arrival until so much time has passed they assume they have died, having no closure. It must be heartbreaking for any parent to be subjected to such unfair treatment. For as long as any*

Afghan can remember, the past thirty-five years have been tragic, unfair, and disappointing. Anywhere Afghans run, death is most definitely waiting for them.

The truck makes it to Pakistani territory without incident. The picture of the young dead men plays over and over in Nick's mind.

The next day, the old, beat-up truck makes it to a Pakistani town. This is the first time Nick has seen people, shops, and restaurants in days.

The kingpin walks to the back of the truck and asks Nick to get off. "We are going to spend the entire day here. We are going to a hotel room. It belongs to a friend, so we are going to be safe here. Since it will take less than a day to get to Kandahar, we are going to leave in the morning tomorrow. When you get to your room, I want you to bring your costume to me. I will stay in the room next to yours."

I don't think the drug man trusts me with his money, Nick thinks to himself. There must be over fifty million dollars in that one suit. It is this kind of drug money that has funded the Taliban for the past several years. This is only one drug run covering one region of the world. The drug business is worth many billions if it is calculated accurately, counting all Afghan regions distributing all over the world. Sadly, it is this drug money that has defeated the forty-four-country coalition in Afghanistan.

Nick finally gets the chance to take a shower after three days. He is glad he is out of the heavy suit. However, his entire body is covered with a rash from sweat and the extremely hot weather. He is tempted to scratch like a madman, but he knows if he does, it might get infected.

One day and one night in an air-conditioned room feels really good. Fresh food is also a blessing to receive after three days of eating MREs.

The next day, Nick is ready for the next and final leg of his journey. This leg will take him closer to his beloved wife, Shaista. He is happy and upbeat this morning.

The drug lord knocks on his door. "Here is the suit. Put it back on. I want to tell you something. The Afghan government is about to fall. Things aren't so great there. The Americans are about to pull out completely. At this point, no one knows what is going to happen next."

Poor Charlie was right, Nick thinks, disappointed and shaking his head. *He told me what was going to happen two years ago. Now, the entire world will witness how bad American decisions have finally caught up to them.*

Nick puts the suit back on and is once again on his way, entering one of the most dangerous parts of the world. Despite the dangers ahead, where the Afghan government is about to fall and the Americans are about to exit Afghanistan, Nick in his heart believes he is one step closer to seeing his beloved wife Shaista.

What will I say to her? Is she expecting me? Nick thinks. He is lost in his own world. Most of the time, he doesn't even notice or care about what is happening around him. All he wants is to see Shaista.

The truck finally makes it to the Afghan border. The devastation is difficult not to notice. The Taliban once again controls most of southern and eastern Afghanistan. The drug lord is known by most Taliban leadership. No one is to bother him, ask him what he is carrying, or where he is going. This is his territory. This is where he is not a drug lord—he is king; he is God; he is respected like a great leader. He is the reason the Taliban are about to rule the country once more.

As they drive further into the city, Nick notices that American helicopters are busy evacuating the last American soldiers from KAF. The scene is very familiar to Nick. It reminds him of the Vietnam era with American helicopters taking off from rooftops. He is stunned to see it happening for real. History is repeating itself.

The truck finally enters a compound right in the middle of the city, the same part where Nick was snatched two years ago. The location sends a chill through his body, the same as when he was first abducted by Molawee Satar, except this time, the streets are full of police and Afghan army uniforms—those who managed to get away. The unfortunate ones have been hanged by the Taliban on every intersection to show the people who is boss.

"We are at our final destination," the drug lord tells Nick. "I want you to spend the night here, and I will send you to Uruzgan in the morning."

Nick can't wait until tomorrow. He wants to go now. He has sacrificed his entire life to be able to touch, kiss, and smell Shaista once more. He is so close, he can almost feel her.

"I must go right now. My family is in danger," Nick tries to argue.

"I cannot guarantee the safety of my men who are my cousins. You have been a great support to our cause, and I want to make sure you get home safely. Take my advice, and I promise I will get you home before lunch tomorrow," the drug lord assures Nick with a firm insistence.

Nick really wants to walk out and go home. However, there are no taxis after dark, and he could get killed for no reason in such a volatile atmosphere. Nick is escorted by some men to a guestroom.

The compound feels like a city within the city. It is huge and modern, the best of the best that drug money can buy. There must be fifty or so diesel generators taken from various American bases piled up in the corner, which without a doubt is a sobering reminder of American defeat. Nick at last takes off the suit and gives it to the drug lord. He feels free and about 120 pounds lighter. He can hear heavy gunfire close by. The gunfire quiets down in the early hours of the morning.

The next morning, Nick wakes up at three o'clock, anticipating the trip to Uruzgan. He has had barely any sleep. He is going to wait at least for daybreak. He lies back in his bed in the dark room for two more hours. He plays the scene of going to Uruzgan and seeing Shaista after so long over and over in his head. His imagination runs like that of a young man who is madly in love for the first time. He gets a rush in his gut every time he thinks about arriving at Gulbaz's house.

Nick hears someone walking toward his room, shuffling along. Nick immediately gets up. Sure enough, someone knocks, and Nick opens the door.

"Are you ready? The fighting has slowed down in the city. This is a good time to leave because we don't know what is going to happen half an hour from now."

"Yes, I'm ready," Nick replies. "Let me get my bag. I'll be right outside."

Nick grabs his bag and runs out to the car. It's the same driver who drove him all the way from Bandar-e Abbas. Nick is happy to see him because this driver knows his way around the area and in fact knows his way around many nations.

"Are you ready to go home?" the driver asks Nick.

"Oh yes. I have waited for this day for a long time. Let's go," Nick replies with a smile.

As the driver is about to leave the premises, the drug lord waves at him to stop. "I think my boss wants to talk to you," the driver tells Nick.

"You are finally ready to leave," the drug lord says.

"Yes, and I have you to thank for getting me this far," Nick replies. "I could not have done it without you."

"As a matter of fact, I want to thank *you* for bringing our package home safely. I want to extend my hand in friendship and tell you to call me whenever you need anything. And by the way, my name is Arbab." The drug lord finally introduces himself, knowing Nick is no longer a threat to his operation. He also knows that, in Afghanistan, there are not many who are going to challenge him. "Here is a little something for your courage and honesty." Arbab pulls out a thousand dollars in one-hundred-dollar bills, folded neatly.

Nick takes the money because refusal could lead to hard feelings in Afghanistan. Regardless of Arbab being a drug lord, he still has the hospitality typical of an Afghan. *My first illegally earned money*, Nick thinks as he puts the money in his vest pocket.

The driver starts moving, and Nick waves good-bye to Arbab. A guard opens the large gate, and once again, Nick is out there on his own without any protection except the well-known Toyota Land Cruiser that is familiar to many in the area.

This time, Nick has left without any government protection, and this time, he is on his own—no tags and no IDs—and with his long beard, no one knows who he really is. This time, no one is going to look for him or try to rescue him. He is out here in the most dangerous part of Afghanistan without a single friend or family member. Nick has no fear, for he is blinded by his overwhelming love for his beloved wife, Shaista. Nothing can stop him now—nothing.

CHAPTER FOURTEEN

The Bitter Truth

For the first time, he is alone where no law exists in any way, shape, or form. People can get killed over nothing, and in his case, he could become a hostage again just like that. However, what he has in his arsenal this time is a very good understanding of the Afghan culture and some language ability.

After a four-hour drive over the same route he traveled blindfolded when Molawee Satar captured him, except with many twists and turns to avoid detection, Nick finally makes his way to the village where his troubles began.

He is overly excited as he gets closer and closer to what he has been away from for a long time. Anyone who is an outsider will be noticed by the villagers, and Naikee is not an exception. But he feels that every step he is taking puts him closer to Shaista. He doesn't notice anyone noticing him.

Nick sees the old shop where he was held for many months. The sight sends a chill through his body and reminds him of the hard days he endured in that mud hut.

Kids in the village usually stop playing when they hear a car coming by. Like curious children everywhere in the world, they wave to him and are glad to see a car in their village.

Nick points to Gulbaz's compound and tells the driver to stop there. The driver pulls over by the house and asks Nick if he needs anything.

"You have been very helpful," Nick replies. "Thank you for getting me home safely."

"I will wait for you to knock on the door. When the door opens, I will leave."

Nick jumps out of the SUV and grabs his black duffel bag that has traveled thousands of miles since he left home. Is this going to be the final destination for Nick and his tired, black duffel bag? He knows that staying in Afghanistan is not an option for him. He must leave this country as soon as he gets his beloved wife.

Nick knocks on the door with his heart beating very quickly. The Kuchi dog starts barking. A voice from the other side calls, "*Tsaoke yee?* [Who are you?]"

"*Naikee yem. Darwaza khelasa kera, Gulbaz mama.* [I am Naikee. Open the door, Uncle Gulbaz.]"

Naikee can hear Gulbaz laughing on the other side of the door in complete disbelief. One side of the large, heavy wooden door opens, and Gulbaz opens his arms to receive Naikee.

"*Kapera, te la de kom khewa raghlai?* [Infidel, how did you get here?]"

"It is a long story. I will tell you later."

Naikee waves to the driver to leave, and the driver departs, waving back.

Naikee wants to go to the main house as soon as possible. Gulbaz keeps asking questions, but Naikee is not interested in them. He wants to see Shaista as soon as possible.

Shaista runs out of the house and, despite her father's presence, runs into Naikee's arms. Gulbaz is a wise man. He knows this is their time. She has suffered a great deal, and any cultural irregularities are accepted in a moment like this. After all, this is her husband, and nothing is wrong with her showing real emotions.

She is sobbing, and Naikee is crying with her.

"Where were you?" she asks. "You told me, 'I will be back soon.' Well, soon turned to months."

"I know, I know. But I am here now," Naikee replies.

"I think we should go inside the main house," Gulbaz says. "I don't want anyone to know you are here again. I don't want people listening to you two. Please, let's go home, and you two can talk inside."

Toor, Gulbaz's blind son, is also standing nearby and calls Naikee's name. Naikee runs and picks him up. Toor puts his head on Naikee's shoulder with a big smile on his dirty face.

It is already lunchtime. Shaista brings everyone food, laying it neatly on the floor on top of the *desterkhwan* (cloth or plastic table cover laid on the floor or carpet to eat on). Her hands tremble from overexcitement. She sits close by her husband with her brother in her lap. No one wants to eat because it is such a happy time.

After lunch, Gulbaz asks Naikee what took him so long to come back. Naikee realizes that no explanation of his life will satisfy a simple man such as Gulbaz or a simple woman such as Shaista. He mostly avoids telling them about his life in America and tells them what he went through to get here from Dubai.

The story amazes Gulbaz. However, Naikee's story really impresses Shaista. She knows that all the sacrifices Naikee has made have been for her. The afternoon turns to evening, and none of them notice what time it is. Naikee excuses himself. He wants to go to his old room. He really wants to spend more time with Shaista, to tell her about how much he has missed her.

That night, Naikee and Shaista are inseparable. She holds both of his hands, putting them on her face and smelling them. Naikee holds her in his arms, rubbing his eyelids on her face. They talk, just talk.

The night turns into morning. They did not want to go to sleep because both felt that if they did, it might be a dream. If it was a dream, they really wanted to stay in it forever.

One thing Naikee understands and has no illusions about is that this dream can turn into a nightmare soon if he decides to stay here. He needs to state his intentions to Gulbaz and Shaista now before it's too late to go anywhere. The unpredictable situation in Afghanistan can quickly turn worse. If the already intense civil war takes a turn for the worse, he may be killed here or, worse, become a bargaining chip among different groups of Taliban and Al-Qaida.

Before breakfast, Naikee says to Shaista. "I want to take you away from here. This place is not safe. We can all leave this place, and once things get better, we can return."

Most decisions are made by men in Afghanistan. Shaista really does not have much say in it. She will go anywhere her husband takes her. One thing he is sure of—she does not want to be left here again without Naikee.

At breakfast, Naikee tells Gulbaz his intentions.

"She is your wife. You are free to take her anywhere you are going. I am not leaving. Things will get better here soon, *inshallah*. I have faith in God."

Of course, this is a typical response from a typical Afghan man. Naikee does not want to pressure Gulbaz into leaving. His father-in-law will not fit anywhere except in Bazan Kelai, where he was born and where he wants to die. He probably will be forced to remarry for the sake of his blind son because he will not be able to take care of the boy or himself.

"I know you are a good man. You will take good care of my daughter. You have my blessing, and God be with you, my son."

Naikee understands that the news sends an electric bolt through Shaista's veins. At this point, she does not have any doubts about how much Naikee loves her. She for the first time will leave her father's house. She has never left the house or put her foot outside the door. This will be an electrifying moment for her.

"You must be patient for a few days," Gulbaz insists to Naikee. "I want to find someone for you to get you out of Uruzgan on to Herat or Farah. Things are kind of bad out there right now. My friends will protect you around Uruzgan, but once you leave the area, you need to be very careful."

The fighting has spread out of control all over Afghanistan. The central government has lost control in most parts of the country. The very fragile peace that was being held together by foreign powers for many years now has created a large vacuum for warlords, drug dealers, the Taliban, and Pakistani forces to gain control of the government buildings. No one really knows what they are fighting for except the Pakistani forces, who once and for all will take control of southern and eastern Afghanistan to add it as their sixth province, and with the Afghans' disunity, the entire country will soon fall under Pakistan's control.

This is the most dangerous time for anyone to be living in Afghanistan. People get killed on the streets by stray bullets as they are forced to find food. People are being forced to go out of their homes because of the sheer need for survival, not on needless outings in search of trouble.

Naikee is aware of the dangers. He is not willing to take a chance staying in Afghanistan. There are still some foreign forces left in the country, protecting their last remaining personnel. This may be the best time for Naikee to get out once and for all. Once all foreign forces leave, the fate of the country is in the hands of the unknown.

"I think I will leave tomorrow. I have been spared so far. I cannot take a chance on things getting worse," Naikee says, reasoning with Gulbaz.

The next day, Naikee tells Shaista to fit all her belongings with his into the one duffel bag he brought with him. He wants to travel lightly because they may be forced to walk some distance.

It has been Shaista's dream to one day leave her father's home with Naikee. However, now that the moment has arrived, it does not seem so easy. She is going to leave the only house she has ever known, the place she was born in. The most difficult part is leaving Toor, her blind brother, whom she has practically raised as her own son. Naikee notices her sadness but does not want to ask her about it as she might not want to leave, which would complicate things even more.

The moment for good-byes arrives. Naikee hugs Gulbaz and does not have the stomach to say good-bye to his blind brother-in-law. Toor may be blind, but he can hear everything very well. He is glued to Shaista but is not yet crying. The tense moment will leave a horrifying memory in everyone's mind. But good-byes must be said, and Naikee and Shaista will have to leave soon.

Shaista kisses her father's hand and asks for his blessings. Toor starts screaming when his father pulls him off of Shaista. She is the only woman he has known as a mother. The scene is unbearable. Shaista is sobbing under her mustard-colored *burqa*. For the first time, she puts her foot outside her father's house. The type of feeling she imagined does not happen. She wants to get far away as soon as possible so she cannot hear Toor's loud cry.

Naikee and Shaista have to walk a good mile to the nearest bazaar. If they are lucky, a taxi may be waiting there. Otherwise, they may have to return home.

The intense fighting usually stops during the day. However, small arms fire can be heard in the distance and sometimes close by. Daytime is the best time to move around, and Naikee wants to make it to a town before nightfall. Luckily, an old Russian Volga taxi from the 1950s is parked close to a tea shop.

"You wait here," Naikee tells Shaista. "I am going to find the taxi driver."

Shaista reluctantly agrees to wait far from the tea shop so other men cannot see her. Naikee finds the driver, who is as old as his car. However, Naikee prefers an older driver to a younger one because a young driver most likely would sell them to an armed group.

"Brother, how much would you charge me to go to Herat?"

"What the hell business do you have in Herat at a time like this?" the driver asks.

"I am visiting some family in Herat. Can you please take me there?"

"Yes, sure, but I am not taking Afghan rupees. I only take dollars. Do you have some?" the driver asks.

Although mentioning dollars is automatic suicide, the driver is old, and Naikee doesn't have any other choice.

"Yes, I do, but please don't mention it out loud."

"I want to get paid now before I even let you sit in my car. Let's go. And I see you have a woman traveling with you."

Naikee pulls out the money he earned from his drug-money run.

"How much?"

"Eight hundred dollars."

"Really? Herat is not even that far!" Naikee protests.

"Well, first of all, yes, it is very far, and second, you have the choice to catch the next taxi. Do you know how much a liter of gas costs? Twenty-five dollars—if you are lucky to find any fuel at a time like this," the driver says sarcastically.

Naikee pays the taxi driver, and they set off on their way to Herat. The old taxi smell, a mixture of gas and old upholstery, is not very comforting to Naikee. This old and tired car could break down at any moment.

Coming to Afghanistan this time has presented challenges, but at least Naikee was on his own, and he has a woman traveling with him now in hope of getting out of Afghanistan. The oddness of the situation could not be more apparent—a couple in love, a wife and a husband with absolutely nothing in common, traveling in the most dangerous and lawless part of the world with no plans in front of them.

The taxi driver is not able to find a working gas station to fill up. He makes a stop every hundred miles or so to find someone for more gas. Every stop takes at least two hours to find the right person and finally for the gas to reach the tank. The normal ten-hour drive stretches to twenty or more before the taxi reaches its final destination. Every stop carries a great amount of danger for Naikee and Shaista. Shaista holds Naikee's hand tightly. The simple touch of her hand comforts her husband. He at times forgets where he is and what danger he is going through.

After ten hours of stopping in many places for gas, it starts to get dark. The old taxi driver decides to stop for the night.

"I am going to stop for the night. I cannot stop at the nearby town because someone may rob us. I know a safe place down the road under the trees where no one will detect us."

Naikee agrees with the driver and slowly explains the situation to Shaista. Shaista does not say a word and squeezes Naikee's hand in agreement. The taxi slowly stops under the trees with its lights off in total darkness.

"Do not turn on any lighters, flashlights, or any kind of lighting because it can give away our position to thieves and the like," the taxi driver pleads.

"Don't worry," Naikee assures the driver. "We are not carrying any of the things you just mentioned."

The driver exits the taxi and opens the trunk. He comes back with water in a plastic container that once held engine oil, and he also has some flatbread wrapped in a piece of white cloth.

"Here is some food and water if you two are hungry," the driver says to Naikee.

"Thanks. We have food, but we will need some water," Naikee replies.

Naikee gives the plastic container to Shaista so she can have a drink of water. She drinks straight from the container because there are no glasses. Naikee also drinks from the engine oil container. Shaista pulls a piece of flatbread from the duffel bag. They both take a piece and eat it slowly.

The driver excuses himself and tells Naikee, "I am really tired. It is very hot, and I am going to sleep outside on top of the car. You two can open the windows and sleep inside the car."

Naikee agrees with the driver. He is happy to spend the night anywhere with Shaista. Shaista leans her head on Naikee's shoulder. Naikee gives her a kiss, assuring her that everything is going to be okay. The snoring from the driver sleeping on top of the car keeps them both awake for hours. They lose track of time and fall asleep sometime late in the night.

The taxi driver wakes up before dawn. After putting his sleeping bag away, he wakes Naikee and Shaista. This is Shaista's first time away from home. She wakes up breathing heavily at first, as she has no idea where she is. After a couple of seconds, Naikee's presence gives her comfort, and once again she holds his hand very tightly like a child holding her mother's hand at the fairgrounds.

The driver greets both as he enters the car. "We need to get going and make it to Herat before dark tonight. We are going to face the same hurdle with finding gas, and I want to give us a head start."

"How far is Herat from here?" Naikee asks.

"I would say about the same distance we covered yesterday," the driver replies.

The driver cranks the old, tired carbureted Russian-made Volga while pumping the gas. The taxi refuses to start. The driver makes several more attempts, but the old car does not cooperate the way the driver hopes. By this time, the carburetor is flooded with gas, and the driver faces three problems. First, he has to wait for the flooded carburetor to clear out; second, the battery has died; and finally, repeated cranking will attract unwanted attention.

Naikee can see the driver is getting tense by how he is getting in and out of the car, trying to find a way to start the car as soon as possible. Naikee has to interfere because they can put their heads together to find a solution before someone robs them or, worse, robs and kills them here in the middle of nowhere.

"Can I help?" Naikee asks the driver.

"What do you know about cars?" the driver replies.

"I owned a car before. I know a thing or two about them," Naikee replies.

"Well, here's what we have to do. You need to hand crank the car since the battery is dead."

"I do what?"

The driver walks to the back of the car. He opens the trunk, pulls out a rod, and hands it to Naikee.

"Oh, that!" Naikee realizes the old car can be turned on even without a starter. He has never seen anyone do it, but he remembers seeing it on TV on *The Three Stooges* when Moe, Curly, and Larry start their Model-T Ford.

114

"Here is what we are going to do. You crank the engine, and I will try to get it started," the driver tells Naikee.

Naikee hand cranks the engine several times. Finally, on the fifth try, the car turns over. The driver gets out of the car, puts the rod in the trunk, and tells Naikee to jump in quickly.

The old car once again is on its way to Herat. The taxi driver stops in the next town to find gas. The pattern repeats itself several times until the old taxi has finally made it to Herat.

Herat has always been a model city compared to the rest of Afghanistan. However, the recent chaos has not spared Herat, either. What surprises Naikee is that Iranian government militiamen are everywhere in the city. This part of the county is controlled by the Iranian government, or in other words, they have claimed this part to be their own as most of Afghanistan has been claimed by its neighbors and cut into pieces.

The infighting, tribalism, racism, lack of loyalty to country, working for and serving neighbors as servants and slaves, and lack of education have finally caught up with the Afghans, Naikee thinks. A country that once conquered Iran and India is now cut into pieces and unable to even defend itself. Once an existing nation, soon it will no longer appear on any map as a country. Those who served as slaves—known as the party of eight, the Taliban, the Northern Alliance, the Hazaras, the Pashtuns, and the Tajiks—have finally sold their county to their masters and will forever serve as slaves and servants. *What a shame,* Nick thinks.

The taxi driver stops on the outskirts of the city. "This is as far as I will go. I don't know what is out there, nor do I want to know. I wish you both good luck, and stay safe." The driver reads a prayer and wishes them both lots of luck.

Yes, Naikee will need all the luck in the world to get out of here. He doesn't know anyone. He doesn't speak Farsi or Dari, and soon it will be dark.

As difficult as it is to leave the safety of the old taxi that has kept them both alive for the past two days, along with the help of a wise taxi driver, Naikee is very limited in his choices and reluctantly leaves the vehicle. He may never see the kind driver again.

CHAPTER FIFTEEN

Awkward Moments

Naikee and Shaista walk along the boulevard alone. For Naikee, this may be the most awkward moment of his life. He walks with his entire life in his duffel bag and an Afghan following him in her mustard-colored *burqa* one step behind. He does not know where he is going or what he is going to do next.

It is getting dark, and soon Naikee must find a place to stay. In a city where he does not know anyone and with no operating or even existing hotels, his best bet is to find a mosque to spend the night in. It is probably the safest place to sleep. He walks toward a mosque in the distance.

When they arrive, it is pitch dark. Naikee knocks on the mosque's door. No one answers at first. He knocks for a second time, and still no one answers the door.

I have never seen a mosque completely locked and everyone gone home, Naikee thinks.

It must be the eighth or the ninth time that Naikee knocks when someone on the other side of the door finally asks, "Who is it, and what do you want at this time of night?"

"I am a traveler, and I have nowhere else to go. Can I please spend the night here?"

"This is not a hotel. Go find a hotel somewhere."

"If I were by myself, I would have slept right outside. But my wife is with me. I can't sleep outside. Can you please find it in your heart to let us stay here tonight?"

The man on the other side of the door does not say anything for a moment. Naikee can hear his steps going away from the door. Soon the man appears on the rooftop to make sure Naikee is telling the truth. He walks back and opens the door.

"*Aslaumalikum*," Naikee greets the mullah in charge of the mosque.

"*Walikum asalam*. Don't you have any family, relatives, or friends around here? It is very dangerous walking around with a woman."

"No. If I did, I wouldn't have bothered you," Naikee replies.

"I don't have any food. I can bring you water if you want."

"Water is fine. We don't need any food," Naikee says.

"You need to be out of here before the morning prayer," the man rudely demands.

"Don't worry. We will be out of here before the morning prayer," Naikee says politely.

The mullah leaves and returns with a water pitcher, leaving it on the floor. He leaves again without saying a word.

Shaista again pulls out a piece of flatbread, which is very stale by now. The last time they had anything to eat was the night before, also just a piece of flatbread. Naikee leans his duffel bag against the wall. He puts his head on the bag while looking up at the ceiling. He asks Shaista to lean back and make the best of this night. She also puts her head on the black duffel bag, facing Naikee.

"We have some more very hard and uncertain nights ahead of us," Naikee tells Shaista. "I want to promise you that once we are in Dubai, I will make everything all right. I want to buy a house for you. I want to buy a car for you. And we are going to have lots of kids! What do you think?"

"I don't want anything worldly," Shaista replies. "However, I want to be with you under any circumstances, and yes, I want to have lots of kids."

They both heave a long sigh in hopes of better days ahead. Naikee holds Shaista's hand tightly. They face each other in the totally dark room, pretending they can see each other. They fall asleep daydreaming about well-being, security, and a dignified life in the coming months and years.

The next morning, the mosque custodian is standing right over the couple, silently watching them sleep. Naikee can feel him even without seeing him. He wakes up right away and stands up.

"Is it time for us to move on?" Naikee asks.

"Yes. I want you to leave before the morning payer. Not that anyone will show up to pray—things are so unsafe, no one wants to leave their homes before sunrise. But I have been told not to let anyone sleep overnight in the mosque."

"I understand what you are saying," Naikee says. "I appreciate your letting us stay here last night. I don't know what I would have done if you had refused to let us stay here. Thanks."

"I want you to fill your water bottle because you may not find any out there. I wish I had food to offer you, but with the fighting going strong outside, I don't know when my own next meal will be," the man says sadly. "All I can say is, God bless you, and I hope for this county the best of luck because we all need it."

Naikee picks up his duffel bag, and he and Shaista leave the mosque while daybreak is barely above the eastern horizon.

There are no cars on the nearby road. Naikee decides to wait for a while and start moving once there are people around. He and Shaista will have to walk many miles before he can figure out a way into Iran. Around seven, shopkeepers start opening their stores. Naikee can smell fresh bread from the nearby bakery. He decides this might be a good time to start moving since the day is still young, and their safety can be compromised if they wait too long.

Shaista has never asked for anything since they were married. "Naikee?" She does not find the courage to ask him for what she really wants. "Oh, it is nothing. Nothing important."

Naikee notices her eyes gazing toward the bakery. He is so consumed by the idea of getting out of Afghanistan that he has completely forgotten about the little things that make people happy—especially Shaista, whom he feels overwhelming love for, the love he has gambled everything for. This is the moment in the now, and this is the moment they will remember forever.

"Let's go. I think I know what you were going to ask me," says Naikee.

Shaista feels quite embarrassed and walks right behind him.

"You sit here," Naikee says. "I am going to see what I can find for us to eat." He leaves her with a smile, as women aren't allowed in the eating area of the bakery.

Naikee walks back with two fresh flatbreads and a small tea kettle with two cups filled with sugar. "This is all they have in this place," he tells Shaista.

"I wanted us to sit for a while and talk," says Shaista with a smile. "We haven't had any time to spend together since you returned. I just wanted a little moment for us to be together."

"I know," Naikee replies.

This moment will last for as long as they are together. But the brief moment must come to an end, and Naikee still needs to find a way to get across the border to Iran and on to Dubai.

Naikee had a little chat with the baker when he ordered food. The baker told him to follow the same road they were on for a couple of miles. "Find the bus station, and in the same place, you will find people who are going across the border on a daily basis," the baker said.

Soon, Naikee and Shaista are once again walking on the road's shoulder. The bus station appears in the distance with bright, colorful paintings on the sides of the minivans and large passenger buses.

The little chat they had has given Shaista an extra boost of energy to once again keep up with Naikee's fast-paced walking. Normal travel to Iran has come to a full halt since the near collapse of the Afghan government. Buses and minivans are parked idle, hoping to find enough passengers to take anywhere. However, there are those old Toyota pickups driven by smugglers and drug runners that will take some passengers for extra cash and perhaps a cover story, especially if a woman is on board. A woman's presence always creates a sense of urgency, and in this case, taking a woman across the border to Iran will deter the border patrol from an intensive search. For a smuggler, it is a golden opportunity to pick up a woman passenger in such an uncertain time as this.

Naikee knows the drill. He is not going to ask anyone for a ride. He wants a driver to approach him. This way, Naikee may have a good chance to hitch a free ride since his money is about to run out. Naikee looks from the corner of his eye, spotting some pickup trucks not too far but close enough. A bunch of them are parked here and there in and around the bus stop/truck stop. A driver's assistant seizes the moment, as they have been trained to be persistent and make a move before another driver's assistant does. Naikee knows from his work in the UN how driver assistants become the driver and the child abuse and sexual abuse that take place. Drivers' assistants are young boys who are hoping to become drivers one day. In many instances, they may be related to the driver or to the owner of the vehicle, or the driver may be keeping the boy for his sexual pleasure. Whatever the case may be, drivers' assistants rarely get paid. They have been hired on the promise of becoming a driver one day and are fed three square meals a day.

A young boy approaches Naikee, conversing in his broken Dari with a thick Pashtu accent. "Looking for a ride?"

Naikee does not answer. The persistent boy asks again, "Are you looking for a ride across the border?"

Naikee answers back in Pashtu with his precise Kandahari Pashtu accent. "You are far from home. What are you doing here?"

The clever young boy knows what Naikee has just implied. With a silly smile, the boy says, "You are very far from home, too, and we all have to earn a living no matter where we are."

Naikee thinks to himself, *Don't let my Kandahari accent fool you. You have no idea how far I am from home.*

"I don't have any money," Naikee says.

"I will charge you half the normal fare," the boy replies persistently, as he does not want to pass up this passenger accompanied by a woman.

"Well, another driver is going to take me for free," Naikee says.

The young boy nervously walks away from Naikee to ask his driver if it's okay to take him and his woman passenger across the border. In a split second, another boy starts running from not too far away to speak to Naikee. But the first young boy spots the other driver's assistant from the corner of his eye and makes a quick U-turn. He knows very well that this may be the only chance he gets. He says to Naikee, "Okay, I will take you for free. Let me take your bag." The driver gets the signal and starts his beat-up diesel Toyota pickup.

There are no passengers in the back of the truck. In Afghanistan, it usually would be filled with at least twelve passengers, bags of wheat right in the middle, a dozen chickens, and a goat or two. Naikee and Shaista are able to get a free ride. Naikee knows what these drivers are up to. He and Shaista will make a good physical PR statement in the front seat.

Naikee heaves a sigh of relief as the pickup truck starts moving. Shaista slips her hand from under her *burqa* and holds Naikee's hand without the driver noticing. Every journey takes Naikee closer to where he is going and Shaista further away from her home. However, she will go anywhere as long as she is with Naikee.

After a couple of hours, the driver makes an unscheduled stop. He exits the truck without saying anything and walks toward an isolated shop in the middle of nowhere. After ten minutes of waiting, the young boy jumps from the back as the driver and two other men start loading the truck with what look like bags of wheat. The smell coming from the bags confirms otherwise. Naikee has known all along that at some point he would see or smell drugs in one form or another. The truck is filled beyond its capacity, and the two men sit backwards with their legs dangling from the truck's tailgate. As Naikee predicted, the real journey begins now.

The truck drives the last stretch of supposedly paved road, though it is badly broken with crater-sized potholes. The old, beat-up truck enters an imaginary sandy road known only to experienced drivers. The driver does not carry a map and has never seen or heard of GPS. These drivers drive like flying wild geese and use their natural instincts, like finding their birthplace for the first time after they were hatched from an egg.

The driver gets comfortable. He takes his hat off and pulls an old cassette from the glove compartment. He asks Naikee, "Do you like music?"

"Yes," replies Naikee, unsure if it's a trick question.

The driver slides the cassette into a dusty tape player. The squeaky sound coming from the old cassette player confirms that it still has some life left in it. The blank part of the tape passes through the head of the player. The static sound ensures that Naikee will hear some kind of music pretty soon.

The speakers blast a loud Afghan folk song. Shaista jumps at such loud music. The driver's assistant approvingly bangs on the side of the truck and says, "Louder!"

The driver cranks up the music even more. He plays the same music for several hours, and the cassette tape reverses many times over. There is nothing Naikee can do to stop the ear-piercing music, which he has never liked. Afghan music always sounds out of tune to him. Listening to the same music over and over is unbearable.

This is worse than the waterboarding the Americans use to get information, Naikee thinks. *If I were a prisoner, I would have confessed to everything, even if I wasn't guilty of any crime.*

Somehow, magically, the player stops playing the horrible music. The driver looks at Naikee with a worried look, and Naikee replies with a smile. The driver starts cursing, and Naikee tells him, "We have a woman in the car—a little respect?"

The driver still mumbles curse words as he pulls the tangled tape from the player and shakes his head in disappointment. He turns to Naikee and asks, "Can you sing? I will clap."

"No, I don't know how to sing," Naikee replies.

The driver continues driving silently. The rough ride in the old diesel truck makes everyone tired and sleepy.

Shaista leans against Naikee. She is about to fall asleep. The front seat is very tight. The stick touches Naikee's leg every time the driver shifts. Naikee wants to let Shaista lean on him and get some sleep, but there is no room to spare.

Naikee also dozes off momentarily. He always has the same disturbing dream about his daughter, Ashley, when he is under a lot of stress. The dream is about Ashley running toward him. He wants to hold her and comfort her, but he cannot reach her no matter how hard he tries.

The driver slows down, and Naikee wakes up, wiping drool from the side of his mouth. The driver makes a ninety-degree sharp turn to the left.

"What's wrong?" Naikee asks.

The driver screams in Pashtu, "*Irani sarhadi!* [Iranian border patrol!]"

"What are you going to do?" Naikee asks.

"I will drive fast!" the driver nervously answers.

"That is your plan?"

The driver does not even answer. Shaista does not know what is going on. However, she can sense distress on her husband's face. The two armed men in the back get the message when the driver makes the sudden ninety-degree turn. The Iranian border patrol turn on their lights and approach the truck quickly with sirens blaring.

Shots ring out. The men in the back shoot back. Shaista starts screaming. The driver gets even more nervous and drives out of control. The firefight intensifies, and the border patrol gets closer and closer. They successfully shoot the rear tire of the old, overloaded diesel truck, and it is no longer able to move fast enough. The driver has no choice but to stop, while the engine temperature rises fast, and surrender.

The shooting stops, and there is no sign of the armed men in the back. They have somehow disappeared as if they were ghosts. The driver at this point is trembling and praying at the same time.

"This is not a good sign," Naikee says, holding Shaista's hand tightly.

The border patrol shouts in Farsi for everyone to get out of the vehicle. No one at this point has a choice. The driver gets out first, followed by Shaista, still holding Naikee's hand, from the right side of the old truck.

"Don't worry. I am here," Naikee assures Shaista.

Everyone is ordered to walk far from the old truck and hold their hands in the air.

"Hold your hands in the air like I am," Naikee tells Shaista.

"Why?" Shaista asks.

"Please don't ask why. Just do it."

For Shaista, the girl who was born in her father's house and until now never went out of that house, this is beyond her comprehension. She reluctantly raises her hands in the air, weeping because part of her traditional dress is on display for everyone to see. This is the most humiliating moment of her life. Naikee knows what is going through her mind but cannot do a thing about it.

The driver calls his assistant to come out with his hands in the air, but he does not get any response. Blood trickles from the side of the truck, confirming that the assistant is either dead or dying.

The border patrolmen rush to the overloaded truck. They really don't have to check the cargo; the smell of Afghan hashish is enough evidence to confirm this is a drug run. The commander of the Iranian border patrol pulls out his pistol and shoots the driver in the head. The commander then approaches Naikee and Shaista. He looks them up and down and then looks at his men. Two of his men grab Naikee. Another man grabs Shaista and pulls the *burqa* off her face.

"Leave her alone, you cowards! She is a woman!" Naikee screams in Pashtu. The border patrolmen do not understand Pashtu, but they understand why Naikee is screaming. The commander takes Shaista's purse from her and empties it on the desert sand. There is not much in her purse—a picture of Naikee and some crumbled Afghan rupees her father had given her when she left home. The commander quickly pockets the worthless Afghan currency.

The patrolmen tie up both Naikee's and Shaista's hands and legs. The commander lights a cigarette and leans on his patrol car. He hands a scooper to his man. Naikee sees the scooper and knows he and his beloved wife will die the most miserable death possible. He witnessed this firsthand in Bandar-e Abbas when he came to get Shaista. The hallmark of the Iranian border patrol—filling the victim's mouth with the desert sand saves a bullet and teaches a lesson to other Afghans. Not that Nick and Shaista had anything to do with the drug run, but their presence in a truck full of drugs automatically identifies them as drug dealers.

Shaista is in total shock. She screams, "Naikee, save me from these monsters! Save me! What are they going to do to me?" Nick knows what is going to happen. He keeps telling her he loves her and nothing else.

Shaista gets the treatment first. Her voice is silenced momentarily, and she manages to spit most of the sand from her mouth. But the second scoop silences her, and the third one ...

Naikee, or Nicholas Blake, cannot believe what has just happened. Nick, the son of Ibrahim, will die in the desert of Iran near the Afghan border. He wants this to end soon. He imagines all of his loved ones smiling upon him, especially his children. Lisa's kind face keeps passing before his face like he remembers it. Shaista is forever silenced. The person he gambled everything for is gone. He does not even want to live anymore.

Nicholas Blake will never be found. No one will look for him or know how he died. For his first wife and his children, this might be the most devastating fact to live with for the rest of their lives. A life without a closure. He will be judged forever as a coward, a selfish and careless person to Lisa and his children. As for Shaista, she did not exist in the first place as a person in Afghan society, and her father will never know what happened to his only daughter.